The Tenant's Guest

The Tenant's Guest

A Pride and Prejudice Variation Novella

LEENIE BROWN

LEENIE B BOOKS

HALIFAX

Contents

Dear Readers,

It all started with a picture of a sunset and a writing exercise on my blog (leeniebrown.com). However, what was supposed to be a few minutes of practice, grew and stretched and became something much larger.

Those writing exercises have now produced several published works, including the one you hold in your hands.

While some things about how I create these stories have evolved since that first writing exercise, the tradition of posting a portion of a work in progress continues each Thursday. In fact, there is a new story posting there now.

Happy Reading!

Leenie B.

Chapter 1

Derbyshire

The sun cast its warm rays over the meadow and danced its way across the stream as a butterfly took an easy but rambling path from one flower to the next. Leaning against the base of a tree, Elizabeth filled her lungs with air and released it slowly. The summer breeze tugged at her bonnet and willingly, she complied to its suggestion by removing her hat and placing it on the ground next to herself. She closed her eyes and listened to the birds sing for a few moments before turning her attention to her purpose for stealing away from the group of picnickers — the two letters in her pocket.

The first letter was well-worn and treasured even though its contents still caused her heart to ache. It had been many months since she had received it, and yet the words, even now, rebuked her for her foolishness. Such arrogance! Such reprehensible behaviour! Surely, she would be never rid of the shame it made her feel.

Carefully, she unfolded the paper, but she did not read it. She did not need to. The words were clearly etched in her mind. She only took it out now, as she did so often, to look at the fine writing and think about the gentleman who had written it.

She allowed her eyes to skim over the writing and then rest for a few moments on the signature. She touched his name reverently, tracing each letter, before refolding the letter and tucking it back into her pocket while chiding herself, as she did each time, about her stupidity in refusing such a man.

If she could but go back... if she could choose her words again...but she could not. What had been said, had been said, and words, once spoken, could not be withdrawn.

She drew the right corner of her bottom lip between her teeth, looked across the meadow toward where she knew Pemberley to be, and sighed a small sigh of regret. Part of her wished to see it and perhaps chance upon its owner, while another part of her would like nothing better than to be much further away from any chance meeting with Mr. Darcy. For such a meeting, should it ever occur, was certain to be strained and would no doubt cause her greater pain by reminding her of exactly who it was she had so soundly refused.

It was difficult enough to hear of him, as she had many times since her arrival at Willow Hall. Each time, she felt a further prick of her conscience. He was a good friend, a well-respected landlord, and a fair and just master. She had heard it all — many times.

Slowly, reluctantly, she withdrew her hand from holding the letter in her pocket.

Lucy Dobney had said Mr. Darcy might arrive before the summer's end. Her husband, Philip, had insisted it would be much sooner. Again, a small glimmer of hope battled with an urge to flee at the thought.

She shook her head attempting to clear her thinking. Her mind had been muddled with confusing and conflicting thoughts ever since the evening before she had received this letter — the night when he had declared himself to her.

Regret once again crept into her mind. Perhaps if she had not been startled by his addresses. Perhaps if she had not heard of his part in separating her sister from Mr. Bingley. Perhaps if she had not had a headache. Perhaps then she would have replied in a kinder, more gentle fashion. She forced away the thoughts. What had been said, had been said. What was done, had been done. It would do no good to dwell on what might have been.

She took one last look towards Pemberley and then broke the seal on the second letter. This letter held the promise of much happier thoughts. It was the first Elizabeth had received from Jane since arriving at Willow Hall. Anxiously, she read through the details of life at Longbourn — the calls that had been made, the new baby born to one of the tenants, Kitty's sighing over the absent officers, and the delicacy of the flowers on the material her mother had chosen for a dress. Elizabeth's eyes raced along, searching for the one thing for which she hoped. She smiled and clutched the letter to her chest when she found it. Jane would be arriving with the Gardiners in less than a fortnight! She knew, just knew, that a trip away from Hertfordshire to a land as beautiful as this was exactly what her sister needed to help heal her injured heart.

"Miss Bennet."

Elizabeth opened her eyes to find Mr. Marcus Dobney standing above her.

"Mr. Dobney," she greeted and made to stand.

"Please stay as you were. I shall join you for a moment if you do not mind." He waited for her to give her consent before taking a seat on the grass near her. "I take it you have happy news?"

"Oh, very." She made no effort to contain her excitement. "My sister Jane is to come with my aunt and uncle."

Marcus removed his hat and placed it near Elizabeth's. "So, our company is not enough to keep you entertained?" He affected a severe look that was somewhat ruined by the twinkle in his eye.

She cocked a brow and gave him an impertinent smile. "Indeed, I find the populace to be quite dull."

"Is that so?" He laughed. "And here I thought you were enjoying your stay at Willow Hall. Mrs. Abbot will be disappointed to hear she has failed at being a hostess, and my sister will be greatly displeased to be thought of as anything less than engaging."

Elizabeth could not help the giggle that escaped her as she imagined Mary Ellen Dobney's displeasure. Miss Dobney was not reserved, and often her emotions were evident to all — even when she attempted to contain them. "I cannot keep up such a charade, sir. It is precisely because I find this place to be so lovely that I am delighted to be able to share it with Jane."

"A fine response," he said and then, leaning a bit closer to her, continued in a loud whisper, "I shall not inform my sister or your hostess of their supposed failings."

She gave a quick bow of her head. "I thank you, kind sir." She looked toward the stream where the picnic blanket was spread out on a flat stretch of grass. "You have not come to tell me it is time to depart already, have you?"

"Ah, so you do enjoy the country, do you?"

"I do."

"Then you are in luck. Mr. Harker will not hear of leaving for another half hour at least. He insists that the air will do him and us much more good than sitting about chatting in the house, and I am inclined to agree. My sister insists that some exercise in the form of a walk be taken and has sent me to retrieve you." He took up his hat and rose.

"A lovely idea. I am very fond of walking," said Elizabeth as she folded Jane's letter and tucked it next to the one that was already in her pocket.

She cast a sidelong look at Marcus and considered him for a moment while putting on her bonnet. He was handsome, his manners were pleasing, and his fortune was not without merit. He would be an excellent match — her heart sighed — for someone. As pleasant as he was, she found him of no greater interest than she had found Mr. Bingley. "Oh," she said as, while rising to her feet, a thought overtook her.

"Is there a problem, Miss Bennet?" Marcus looked at her in concern. "You did not wrench an ankle, did you?"

Elizabeth shook her head. "No, I am perfectly well. I was merely thinking about my sister." She placed her hand on the arm he offered. Marcus may not be what she wished for in a husband, but she would not be opposed to having him for a brother.

"I suppose it is far too impertinent of me to ask of what in particular you were thinking?" He smiled down at her as they walked.

"Too impertinent and a trifle ungentlemanly," she answered with a small laugh.

He gave an accepting nod. "Yes, to my father's chagrin, I have always struggled with being more curious and forward than a proper gentleman should be. And my sister will attest to my tendency toward ungentlemanly behaviour." He smiled. "But she is my sister, and, therefore, I am somewhat exempt."

Elizabeth laughed. "Then, Mr. Dobney, we are much alike, but I shall not admit to unladylike behaviour, for foibles in decorum are more readily dismissed for gentlemen than they are for ladies. However, I will concede that my mother has scolded me on more than one occasion for not holding my tongue." Her brows furrowed for a brief moment. "There was some wisdom in what she said, of course. A quick tongue has the potential to cause irreparable damage." Without thought, her free hand slid inside her pocket and rested against Mr. Darcy's well-worn and much read letter.

"So it does." Marcus' agreement was so soft she barely heard it, and when she glanced at him, he was staring ahead with a pensive look on his face.

"Shall I assuage some of your curiosity by telling you about Jane?" She watched as the corners of his mouth turned up once again and his gaze became less focused on the distance, and for a moment, she wished to ask him of what he had been thinking. But having just informed him that such questions were too impertinent, she thought it best to hold her tongue.

"A delightful idea," he replied, "but perhaps we should wait until we have joined the others."

Since they had nearly reached the group, she agreed.

"Have you had good news?" Cecily Abbot, a lady of about seven and twenty, delighted in having her home filled with people, especially when those people were young ladies she counted as dear friends and relations. She had been anxiously awaiting Elizabeth's reading of the missive. She had speculated about its contents several times since they had left Willow Hall. She was most pleased to have been late in departing, due to an issue with one of her children, for if they had left exactly as they had planned, Elizabeth would not have received the letter until she returned. And such a letter could not be held until later, for it must contain good news.

Elizabeth held out the letter to Cecily. "Yes, it is very good news. Jane shall be travelling with my aunt and uncle." Elizabeth could not help how large her smile grew at declaring such news. It had been lovely of her aunt and uncle to allow her to travel ahead of them when their plans had been altered due to the business at Mr. Gardiner's warehouse increasing and needing his attentions, but she truly did miss Jane.

Mrs. Abbot clapped her hands and accepted the letter, unfolding it to see the good news with her own eyes. "So a week this Thursday?" There was no mistaking the excitement in her voice. "We shall both have our dearest older sisters to keep us company."

She read the letter quickly, exclaiming here and there about some bit of news that the others might enjoy. Then, returning the letter to Elizabeth, she rose from the blanket so that she could join the others on their walk.

"Oh, my. You shall all love Jane as dearly as I do, I am sure," she said to the group. "Am I not correct, Lizzy?"

Elizabeth laughed. "I am rather partial to Jane, so my agreement benefits you little."

"Miss Bennet has promised to tell us all about her sister as we walk," said Marcus. "Perhaps you could assist her, Mrs. Abbot."

"A wonderful idea, Mr. Dobney. I like nothing better than to speak about my favourite people." She turned to Elizabeth. "I am sure that Mrs. Dobney and Mr. Phillip Dobney grew tired of hearing your name as I waited for your arrival." She looked expectantly at her husband, a man six years her senior, who was still lounging on the blanket. "Surely, Mr. Abbot, you are not going to allow me to go away without your company?"

"As shocking as it may be, I think I shall remain here with Mr. Harker." Harold Abbot stretched out his long legs and rested back on his elbows, as he winked at his wife and added, "I will miss you dearly, you know."

"Without a doubt," she replied with a smile.

Elizabeth loved the repartee between Mr. and Mrs. Abbot. They were so very comfortable with each other and those around them. They easily fell into friendship with those they met, and once having fallen into a friendship, they embraced their friends as family — whether they were friends of one day or many years. Such was their attentiveness to their friends that notes would be sent, gifts given, and help extended before so much as a mention of need was spoken. To be honest, it was a skill Elizabeth envied, for although she got on well with most people she met, her disposition was more prone to judge and criticize than to accept.

"You can link arms with me, Mrs. Abbot," said Mary Ellen. "That is if Miss Bennet is content to remain in my brother's care."

There was a bit of a mischievous glint to Mary Ellen's eye and a playful flick of her eyebrow that caused Elizabeth to worry. It was the same as she had seen on more than one occasion when her mother was playing at matchmaking.

"If I had not promised to tell Mr. Dobney of Jane, I should insist upon Mrs. Abbot taking my place." And truly she would have dropped Marcus's arm and insisted Cecily take her place if it had not been for that promise.

"I do not know whether to be flattered or wounded," muttered Marcus.

"Wounded," said his brother, giving Marcus's arm a playful swat.

Elizabeth's face grew rosy. She had not meant for the comment to be anything other than a discouragement to Mary Ellen's scheming.

"Philip," said Lucy softly. "I believe you are making Miss Bennet feel uneasy, and Mary Ellen." She said no more but gave her friend a stern look.

"Forgive me," said Mary Ellen. "I should not have teased."

"Indeed," said her eldest brother. "Mary Ellen is as much a trial to my father as I am at times when it comes to minding our tongues, but we cannot all be as good as Philip."

"I find I am in agreement with you, Marcus," said Lucy, smiling and leaning into her husband's side just a bit more.

The comment sent a chuckle around the group as they set off on what would be a very lovely half hour.

Chapter 2

The Dobney's barouche was the first to arrive at Willow Hall. As they turned into the small circular drive, Elizabeth noted, before her view was obscured, that a fine carriage stood in front of the house. She must not have been the only one to have noticed the carriage, for she heard the hastening of horses from behind them.

"I see the Abbots have a new guest," Mr. Dobney said with a smile.

"Oh, so they have." Mary Ellen waved to whoever was behind their carriage as the horses came to a stop. "Philip and Lucy will be pleased."

Elizabeth wished to turn around and look to see who this newcomer was but did not wish to appear unladylike and so she sat, waiting until Mr. Dobney would hand her out of the carriage after his sister.

"I had not expected to see you for another month complete." Elizabeth could hear Mary Ellen greeting the visitor as she placed her hand in Marcus's and began descending the steps.

"I had not expected to return, but Georgiana was homesick for Pemberley, and so I indulged her."

Elizabeth's step faltered, and she stumbled slightly while her mind flew toward the voice and away from its job of helping her feet reach the ground gracefully. Her heart beat wildly inside her chest. He was here, standing just out of sight behind the raised canopy of the carriage.

"Are you well, Miss Bennet?" Marcus asked in concern.

"I am, thank you. It was just a small misstep." She flashed him what she hoped was a reassuring smile. Her body felt strangely numb while her mind seemed to be running in circles. She did not even notice how Marcus, who was still looking at her in concern, tucked her hand into the crook of his arm to ensure her safety. She was far too busy contemplating the man on the other side of the carriage and attempting to listen to the conversation.

"Oh, that is the best news," Mary Ellen was saying. "She will have to call on us all as soon as she is settled — and you may accompany her if you wish."

There was a small masculine chuckle of amusement in response to the comment, and Elizabeth nearly stumbled a second time. It was a pleasant sound and one she had not heard before. The Mr. Darcy she knew had not once appeared amused. He had been so serious and very ill at ease. But here, she noted as she stepped out from behind the carriage, he appeared to be quite the opposite. Here, he was smiling and relaxed.

"I had anticipated calling on your brothers at least once before returning to my party in London. They will be travelling with me to Pemberley when –" He stopped speaking as Elizabeth approached. "Miss Elizabeth," he said in surprise.

Philip, who had also approached at just that moment, noted the slight stiffening of his friend's posture and the way he fidgeted with his hat as he greeted the Abbots' guest. Shifting his eyes to Elizabeth, he smiled. So that is how it was, was it? Her cheeks were quite rosy, and her eyes were demurely lowered as if afraid to look at the man in front of her.

"Mr. Darcy," she said with as much of a curtsey as one could make when her hand was being held by a gentleman. Her eyes grew wide at the thought, and she tugged her hand away from Marcus as gently as she could. "Thank you, sir," she said softly. "I believe I have recovered."

"You are unwell?" Darcy, without thinking, took a step toward her.

"I merely stumbled, Mr. Darcy." She once again attempted to smile reassuringly.

"You did not injure yourself?" Darcy barely held his place. His every instinct wished to see to her safety, but, he reminded himself, he had not been granted that privilege.

It was as she had feared. The meeting was uncomfortable and with an audience, which made it even more strained. "I am well. It was just a momentary lapse in grace. Fortunately, Mr. Dobney was there to prevent any injury."

Darcy suddenly became aware of the man standing next to Elizabeth. "Marcus," he acknowledged with a nod. The same feelings he had endured when Elizabeth had laughed and talked with his cousin at Rosings, rose within him. Darcy attempted to remind himself that she had refused him, that he had removed her from his heart, but his heart was not listening. Instead, it was demanding that he remove Marcus Dobney from his place at Elizabeth's side. Of course, he would not do such a thing; he had no right or reason for such an action. Again he attempted to remind his heart that it had been rejected.

Philip bit his lip to keep from chuckling and pulled his wife a bit closer to his side as he watched Darcy fight to control himself. "Mary Ellen must cease all attempts to match Marcus with Miss Bennet, or I fear," he whispered, "he and Darcy will be coming to blows."

Lucy, who had also been watching the meeting, looked at her husband, a slight smile tipped the corners of her mouth up showing her delight. "I believe you are right," she whispered in agreement. Then she tipped her head toward Darcy. "You might wish to greet him. It may be the distraction he needs."

Philip winked at her and followed her suggestion. "Darcy, it is a delight to see you." He waited patiently for the gentleman to acknowledge him.

Slowly, Darcy turned toward him, a smile spreading across his face. "Ah, Philip, Mrs. Dobney."

"Lucy," Lucy corrected, "we are among friends. Will you be with us long?"

A short conversation about Georgiana and some estate matters followed this, and Elizabeth was glad for the moment to compose herself. He had greeted her so kindly. Perhaps, she had not completely lost his good opinion. The thought both caused her heart to hurt and flutter in the same rapid beat.

"I take it you have met the Abbots' guest before today." Philip felt Lucy nudge him in the side, but it was too late, the words had already been spoken.

"Yes, I have." Darcy's answer was short, which to anyone who knew the man as Philip and Lucy did was a sign that there was information he did not wish to impart at this time — perhaps later in a more private location, but not as they were in a group.

"My father's estate borders Netherfield," Elizabeth explained, feeling the need to fill the moment's silence that followed Darcy's answer. "It is not more than a three-mile walk."

Her heart was still racing, but her mind had begun to function more normally. They could meet as friends; surely he would be willing to do so. She cast a questioning look towards him, and thankfully, her mind fell upon a topic which might put everyone at ease. "Mr. Dobney, Mary Ellen," she said turning toward them, "Mr. Darcy could tell you about Jane. I believe he knows her to some extent, and his opinions may be less partial than mine, for I do tend to see only the best in her."

Darcy looked startled for a moment. "I know very little of her. I fear I might do her a disservice."

"Not purposefully, I am sure," Elizabeth said softly. "You seem the sort of man who would never injure another without cause. I am not wrong, am I?"

Darcy searched her eyes. Did she mean what he thought? Had his letter served its purpose in correcting her misconceptions? Might she welcome his presence? "You are not wrong."

She smiled and her stomach flipped as he smiled in return and the wall that seemed to part them crumbled at her feet.

"Miss Bennet, Jane," he clarified, "is," he paused, "an angel. She is both beautiful and kind. She seemingly keeps her emotions under good regulation. She did not complain once while she convalesced at Netherfield — and she was quite ill." He tilted his head and looked at Elizabeth. "As far as I could tell, she has but two faults. She is altogether too pleasant, and she smiles too much." He could not help the delight he felt as he saw Elizabeth's brows raise and her eyes sparkle.

"And it is a good thing she does," Elizabeth replied, "or I would not have seen a smile the entire time I was at Netherfield."

Darcy chuckled. "Bingley smiles."

"Very true. I have been corrected once again." She turned to Mary Ellen. "If it had not been for Mr. Bingley, my stay would have been very," she tapped her lip as she considered her choice of description, "dreary."

"Dreary?" Darcy said in surprise.

"Yes, Mr. Darcy, dreary." Elizabeth tilted her head. "Or do you prefer dull, mundane or prosaic?"

"Surely, it was not so bad as that," interrupted

Mary Ellen. "I cannot imagine Mr. Bingley allowing it to be so."

Elizabeth laughed. "Indeed. Mr. Bingley is as lively as he is pleasant."

Darcy agreed with the statement but refused to allow that he, himself, had been dreary. "I was not silent, and I did not stay in my rooms. I think I did an admirable job of being pleasant considering the circumstances." He smiled at Mary Ellen who was looking rather confused. "Bingley's sisters."

Elizabeth heard Marcus groan softly. Apparently, Hertfordshire was not the only place where Caroline and Louisa were not admired.

"Ah, Mr. Darcy," Mr. Abbot exerted himself into the conversation. "It is a pleasure to see you, sir. All is well, if that was the purpose of your call. The fence has been fixed and the sheep are happy for it."

"You must come in and have some refreshment, Mr. Darcy," added Mrs. Abbot. "Travelling even a short distance on such a dry day can make one thirsty."

Darcy bowed and accepted her offer. He would call every day to check on Willow Hall and its tenants if it meant he could spend time with

Elizabeth. He fell into step with her as they entered the house. "Why am I telling my friends of your sister?"

"I have just had the most delightful letter informing me of her arrival in a week's time."

"She is coming to Willow Hall?"

Elizabeth nodded. "She is travelling with my aunt and uncle Gardiner. Aunt Gardiner and Mrs. Abbot are sisters, you see. Uncle had planned to take me with them on a trip around the lake district, but his plans had to be altered. So, I was sent on ahead, and now Jane shall be able to accompany them."

"Will you be staying long at Willow Hall?" he asked hopefully. If she were staying, he might have a chance to convince her of his worth.

"Two months complete."

Darcy looked about the room. The others had taken seats and were in discussion with each other, but he still spoke quietly even though they were a few paces away from the others, standing just inside the door to the room. "Might I call on you and introduce you to my sister?"

A small amount of peace washed over her. He

was not averse to remaining acquaintances. "It would be an honour, sir."

"I must return to London next week, but at the end of the month, I shall return. Georgiana will stay behind at Pemberley. Lucy will see that she is well, and if you will visit, I shall not worry about her being bored or lonely while I am gone."

Elizabeth could hear the care and worry in his voice for his sister.

"You should know," he continued after a short pause, "Bingley and his sisters will be with me when I return."

"Mr. Bingley?" Elizabeth's eyes grew wide, and her hand flew to her heart. "But, Jane...oh." She had hoped that a tour of the country and a stay at Willow Hall might be beneficial to Jane's state of mind, but if Mr. Bingley were to be here...

"That is why I am telling you," Darcy said softly. "Shall we join the others?" He asked motioning toward where a lively story was being shared by Mary Ellen.

Lucy rested her chin on her shoulder and watched Darcy and Elizabeth conversing. It was obvious to her that they were good friends, if not more. She had never seen Darcy stand so close to a lady or speak at such length. Elizabeth must be the lady about whom he had written to Philip. Her brows furrowed. Those letters had not spoken of a happy man. Philip had been quite uneasy about sharing parts of them with her, but he was equally as uneasy about what he feared was his friend's state of mind.

However, there was no sign of that desperate man here. Elizabeth was lovely. It was not hard for her to imagine Darcy losing his heart to such a lady. They would make a good pair. Mary Ellen's laugh brought her back to the conversation. She sighed. Hopefully, Mary Ellen would be content to have Elizabeth for a neighbour instead of a sister, for after the help Darcy had given her in ridding her of her uncle and achieving her current happiness, she would do her best to see the favour returned.

Chapter 3

Darcy paced beneath a large oak tree, stopping now and again to cast a glance down the path toward Willow Hall. Elizabeth had mentioned taking a walk each morning on this path. Being unfamiliar with the area, she dared not venture too far from the house, so Mr. Abbot had shown her this pleasant path that would take her to the lower field where the remains of a wall stood. It was, she said, much better than repeating the same small circuit in the garden. She had laughed at the idea of growing dizzy with all the turning.

Darcy chuckled at the thought as he made a circuit of the tree and then continued pacing. Perhaps he should have told her that he planned to meet her, but the idea had not come to him until last night when he was sitting in his library wishing she was there.

He removed his hat and ran his hand through his hair. He knew it was dangerous to be allowing himself to hope as he was, but she had seemed welcoming yesterday. She had even agreed to meet his sister. Surely, if she were set against him, she would have refused, or so he thought.

Again, he took a circuit of the great old tree, and this time, as he rounded it and faced Willow Hall, he saw her. He immediately put his hat on and then took it off. He ran his hand through his hair once again and replaced the hat, only to remove it a few seconds later as he waited for her to come close enough to greet.

"Mr. Darcy," Elizabeth called, a smile lighting her face as she approached. "I see you still practice the exercise of walking each morning, although, it would seem you have wandered very far from your home."

He chuckled at the teasing tone of her voice. "I was actually riding," he said as she joined him.

She peeked around him. "Is your horse behind the tree then?"

He shook his head and offered her his arm. "No, I left him at the wall and walked up here in hopes of seeing you." He placed his hat back on his head.

"I hope I was not being too forward in doing so. I do not want to intrude on your solitude."

"Your presence is not an intrusion, sir." Elizabeth watched the path before her. If she was to be honest, she had hoped to meet him on her walk, for there were things which she needed to say to him, things that could not be discussed in company, things she had wished to say for months now. "I must apologize," she began.

"No," he interrupted. "You said nothing that I did not deserve to hear."

"That does not make it right," she argued.

"Neither one of us was without fault on that occasion," he conceded. "I had hoped we might move forward as..." He stopped walking and looked at her, the corner of his bottom lip pulled between his teeth in uncertainty. "I had hoped," he began again, "that we might move forward as friends." He noted how the light in her eyes faded and her lips no longer smiled as widely. "I was certain when I left Rosings that I would never see you again, and then yesterday, when you were here, and you welcomed me, I began to hope..." His voice trailed off, but his eyes held fast to hers.

"As friends?" The word dug at her heart.

"It is not what I would truly wish," he said softly, "but, I am determined to be happy with mere friendship if you would allow it."

She tipped her head to the right, and her eyebrows drew together just slightly as she looked at him. "What do you wish?" Her heart drummed fast and heavy in her chest as she voiced the question.

He smiled sadly. "My wishes and desires remain as they were."

Her cheeks reddened, and she had to look away as she asked, "And what if my wishes have changed?" She looked back at him briefly before looking away once again. "Is there any hope that we might ever be more?" She shook her head. "I know I do not deserve it, but might I have a second chance?" Nearly before she had finished speaking the words, she found herself wrapped in his embrace, and then just as quickly, she was standing on the path looking at his back.

"Forgive me. I should not have — "

"I am uninjured, sir," she interrupted.

"But I had no right — " Her smile as he turned toward her snatched all thought from his head.

"I am uninjured, sir," she repeated. "In fact, I

find I am quite well — more well than I have been in months." She began walking for fear that if she stood still he might embrace her once again, which was an action she would happily allow and even return.

Elizabeth heard Darcy's hurried steps as he came to walk beside her. Joining her, they continued down the path for some minutes in perceived silence, but although there was no word of conversation spoken, their closeness and the comfort of such nearness spoke where words could not as each considered the other with varying degrees of delight. Hope filled each heart.

As they approached the wall which stood in the field just beyond where the trees ended, Darcy finally spoke. "You would welcome my addresses?"

She nodded and peeked at him, thankful for the brim of her bonnet that kept him from looking at her directly. It was not that she was necessarily shy, but speaking of one's heart to the object of that heart's desire was naturally uncomfortable when one had never done such a thing before. In fact, this was the first time that Elizabeth's heart had ever desired any person and his good opinion as it desired Darcy and his opinion. "I would. Very much."

Her hands twisted together slightly and her heart kept its loud and rapid beat in her chest as she continued, for though the topic was a new one, she would not retreat from it, no matter how much her mind begged her to do just that. "I have long regretted my words and my refusal. No, do not acquit me of my words or behaviour. I must speak what I have been contemplating." She looked at him, and he nodded. "My discernment of your character was so faulty that I am truly ashamed of what I said."

He held his arm out to her as they exited the trees. "Please?" he pleaded as she looked at his arm with indecision. "I shall control myself," he murmured.

A small giggle escaped her, and she placed her hand on his arm. The contact of her gloved hand on his jacketed arm and the small act of drawing closer to him did nothing to calm the beat of her heart, but it did bring a peace and reassurance to her mind. "Your words were not untrue. My family has its faults, and my standing is not so great as yours. My relatives do not hold titles or large amounts of land. My father, while I love him dearly, is not so attentive to his duties as he should be. He finds too much enjoyment in the follies of not just others but also his family. Though I have tried, I cannot absolve him of his guilt in the behaviour of my mother and youngest sisters. I have attempted since that day when we last spoke in Kent to sway his opinions and provoke him to action, but I have not succeeded."

Darcy did not miss the pain in her voice and, in response, covered her hand with his free one, squeezing lightly in an attempt to comfort her. His comments about her beloved father were the ones which had caused him the deepest amount of regret. Had someone said such things, whether true or not, about either of his parents, he would have been, at least, as angry as she had been.

"The one thing which I still struggle with to some degree is your interference with my sister." She felt his arm tense beneath hers. "I cannot fault you for seeing to the care of a friend, but I cannot forget the despondence of Jane. On this matter, I still find my mind divided." She paused. "As for the last matter," she looked away and shook her head, "my self-reproach is most severe. I know better than to listen to tales and take them as fact without allowing for a careful examination of both sides. How you could ever forgive me for such behaviour only accentuates my deficiency in considering your character wanting."

They had reached the wall by this time and stood there with her hand still clinging to his arm, and his hand holding it there firmly. Neither wished to part from the other even for a moment.

"You need not explain your actions to me," Elizabeth continued. "Your letter has done so each day." She pulled the well-worn paper from her pocket. "It has been both my reproach and my comfort for these many months, for it is both a reminder of my foolishness and a soothing substitute for your presence because it is your voice I hear as I read it." She put the letter back in her pocket. "I have, since the third or fourth reading of your letter, longed to be able to withdraw my refusal, to turn it on its head and happily accept, but I dared not hope for such good fortune until now."

She drew a deep breath and released it, then turning to face him and taking both his hands in hers, she said, "I have been as foolish as any member of my family. I cannot promote myself to you as worthy of your status or your name, and my portion is not great. However, if you will have me, I can promise to always strive to bring you the honour you deserve and to continue to love you as I do now, most ardently."

"I fear I have lied," he said with a smile.

Her brows drew together as she searched his face. Confusion created by the gravity of his words and the joy of his smile was clearly written on her face. He freed one hand from her hold and placed it softly on her cheek. "I have lied," he continued, "for I am uncertain that I can keep myself under regulation when such loveliness stands before me offering herself to me. I can think of nothing in this world that would keep me from accepting you." He brushed his thumb across her cheek. "I would marry you this day, if I were able." His thumb brushed her cheek once more. "But," he continued, "first, I must speak to your father." His eyes grew worried. "Will he allow it?"

A smile lit her face. "If he does not, mention it to my mother, and he shall soon change his mind." She laughed with him at the thought, but then sobering, she added, "I shall write to him, so that he might be assured that this is my wish."

"You truly wish this? You would have me, arrogant man that I am?"

"I would."

He tossed his hat on the ground and taking her face in his hands, bent to kiss her.

The sensation of his lips pressed against hers took Elizabeth by surprise, and without her willing it to do so, her body leaned into him and her arms wound around his waist as if they knew exactly what to do.

It was no wonder some ladies found themselves in compromising positions when their senses were so attacked as to be wholly outside their own power Elizabeth thought, as she stood some moments later, wrapped in Darcy's arms, her head on his chest. Her mind even now knew that standing here, embracing and being embraced, was not proper, but her body was not willing to listen to anything but the beating of his heart, which matched her own rapid pulse. It was with regret that she followed his lead and slowly stepped away from the embrace when finally both hearts had returned to a more normal rhythm.

"I must go on," said Darcy, "and you must return to Willow Hall." His hand caressed her cheek, and his smile looked almost sad. "I will call later at a proper time, if you are agreeable."

She nodded. "I would be happy to receive your call, Mr. Darcy."

"Fitzwilliam." His voice was soft. "You must call me Fitzwilliam for I intend to call you Elizabeth." There was a stubbornness to the set of his mouth and eyes as if he were prepared to defend his decision.

She raised an impertinent brow and attempted to keep from smiling but could not. "Will it not seem strange to the Abbots if we address each other so informally?"

He chuckled. "Indeed it would, but I do not intend to call you Elizabeth save when we are alone as we are now. I have referred to you as such in my thoughts for some months now." He shook his head. "Nay, nearly a year."

"A year?" She looked at him in question, not only because of the length of time that he had considered her, but because in contradiction to his words of needing to leave, he had tucked her hand into the crook of his arm and was walking with her back toward Willow Hall.

"I do not know exactly when I began to think of you in such familiar terms, but I am fairly certain that it was after your stay at Netherfield." He smiled sheepishly at her. "You were charming."

"I was not," she disagreed. "I was disagreeable."

He shrugged. "It was most charming."

She laughed and held his arm more tightly as she stepped towards him as if there was something about his person that drew her to him. "So I have not only promised myself to an arrogant man, but one who finds argument and debate to be charming?"

He nodded. "So it would seem."

She heard him sigh.

"Do you regret your answer?" he asked.

Elizabeth shook her head and then lay it against his shoulder. "Not this time."

The letter in her pocket reminded her of just how fortunate she was to have been given this opportunity to correct her mistake. "I shall never regret it," she added softly.

She smiled as she heard him sigh once again, only this time instead of holding concern, it was an exhalation of peace. So they walked, slowly, toward the tree where he had met her that morning, where he gave her a second kiss, and where he stood watching her until she reached a turn in the path.

As Darcy stood looking at the path where Elizabeth had been, he considered his good fortune in not only having found her again but in being accepted. He wanted to whoop and toss his hat in the air, but that particular article of clothing was still on the ground next to where he had kissed her the first time.

A smile spread across his face. She was his, or nearly so. He would leave early for town so that he would have time to speak with her father, and then, he would plead a need to see his sister to Bingley, so that he might return to Derbyshire sooner than originally planned. And once returned, he would make known to one and all that she was his.

Plans in place, he drew in a deep breath, released it quickly, and headed back to the wall to find his hat and his horse.

Chapter 4

Days passed. Calls were made and received. Friendships were begun and strengthened. Life and love, like the fields where the labourers toiled, blossomed and flourished. All seemed idyllic, but on such serene and happy times, there must of necessity encroach some form of displeasure or discontent. For Darcy and Elizabeth, this came in the form of a necessary separation of a fortnight, which is not so very long — unless one is in love. And Darcy and Elizabeth were in love. Though they had not spoken of such things, even in private, to any of the friends who surrounded them, there was little doubt in anyone's mind that the two were more than mere friends as they claimed.

Darcy's agitation as he prepared to leave nearly a week after his arrival was quite obvious to Philip, who had, at his friend's request, called at Pemberley. He sat silently waiting in Darcy's study as Darcy shuffled papers and muttered under his breath about business that should have been sorted out but was not.

Finally, his desk cleared of all pressing matters, Darcy leaned back in his chair and began the necessary conversation. "I am reluctant to leave."

Philip nodded. "That is obvious."

Darcy raised a brow.

"You become testy when faced with a duty you do not wish to do but feel must be done," Philip explained.

Darcy sighed. "I apologize. I am reluctant to leave Georgiana." It was partially true. "And because of my reluctance, I wish to ask a favour of you." He ran a finger along the edge of a pile of papers on his desk and allowed his eyes to follow it. He could still not speak of his failure in regard to his sister without some degree of shame. "You and Lucy know of the damage done to her last year."

"She seems recovered," said Philip.

"Yes, and I thank you and Lucy for that. Had you not been willing to take her in for those few weeks while a new companion was obtained, I am certain her recovery would not have been so quick."

"I cannot take credit for that, my friend. It was Lucy." He smiled. "Who would have thought that having nearly had her reputation ruined by her uncle would have been a blessing?" And in truth, it was the commonality of having lost parents and been preyed upon by men who should have been trustworthy which had bonded the two ladies together during that time.

Darcy reluctantly nodded his agreement.

"Lucy's father could not prevent her uncle from acting as he did, any more than you could have prevented Wickham's actions. You may be master of a large estate, but you are not God. Therefore, you cannot discern the intentions of any man save yourself." Philip tried to keep his voice from sounding too much like he was delivering a message from the pulpit rather than sitting in the home of a friend, offering encouragement.

"I have tried to believe that," said Darcy, "but the fact remains —"

"The fact remains," interrupted Philip, "that what has happened in the past cannot be undone. Your sister will be well. Lucy and I will see to it."

He leaned forward in his chair, a small smile on his face. "And I do not believe for one moment that it is leaving your sister that has you in such a state. There have been several occasions over the past year when you have left her to deal with business. I do believe, however, that her experience of being taken in during your absence has you worried that the same may happen to Miss Bennet."

The speed with which Darcy rose from his chair and crossed to the window was all the confirmation that Philip needed. He waited patiently for his friend to speak.

"I lost her once." Darcy's shoulders drooped and his voice was soft. "I narrowly survived the experience. I am not sure I would survive a second time."

Philip tipped his head to the side and studied his friend's back. "So she is the lady of whom you wrote?"

Darcy nodded.

"I suspected as much." Philip rose to join his friend at the window. "Do you fear she is inconstant in her affection? Or does she still withhold her heart from you?"

"No," said Darcy, "she has given me no reason

to doubt her, and yet, I do." He expelled a loud breath as he tried to relieve the feeling of guilt such thoughts brought to him. "And I should not."

Philip clapped him on the shoulder. "Do you see the beauty of the garden?"

Darcy gave him a puzzled look.

"An illustration, my friend," Philip answered with a smile before turning his gaze back to the paths lined with blooms and greenery. "The caretaker no longer worries about the growth of the shrubberies or the trees or the flowers, but when they were newly planted, he did. Presently, he tends and nurtures their growth, but he no longer fears they will not bloom. The same is true of love. Although I still nurture the love that I share with Lucy, I no longer fear it will not bloom. However, you are in the first throes of love, so naturally fears will follow." Philip leaned against the window frame. "A little faith is what is needed. Tell me," he continued, "what is the worst that could happen during your absence?"

"Fire, accident, disease — "

Philip held up a hand to stop the flow of disastrous events. "I really should know better than to ask such a question of you." He chuckled.

"Allow me to rephrase my question. Who, in our acquaintance, would attempt to steal her away from you?" He held up his hand again to forestall Darcy's answer. "Wickham is not here, and the only unattached gentleman Miss Bennet knows well is my brother." He lowered his hand.

"There are others in your parish," Darcy protested rather weakly.

Philip shook his head. "Miss Bennet met many of them before you arrived and even with my sister trying to arrange a match between Miss Bennet and Marcus, she has shown no interest in any. In fact, she was quite uncomfortable with all of Mary Ellen's attempts. You have nothing to fear."

Darcy's brows furrowed, and his mouth turned down in a small frown as he thought.

"Lucy and I will do all in our power to see that Miss Bennet is just as attached to you when you return as she is now." Seeing his friend's features did not relax, he added, "I shall write to you straightaway if any new gentlemen enter our neighbourhood. I shall even offer my sister as tribute in Miss Bennet's stead." He lay his hand on his heart and affected a somber expression as he said the last.

Darcy relaxed and shook his head. "You are a good friend." He chuckled. "So good a friend that I will not mention your offer to Mary Ellen."

Philip laughed. "I thank you for that."

~*~*~

Elizabeth folded the letter and dried her eyes. She leaned her head against the tree and looked up into its canopy. She was uncertain how long she had sat there trying to compose herself. Her emotions had been anything but complacent since yesterday. She shoved her handkerchief into her pocket and drew first one deep breath and then another. It would not do to return to the house looking as she imagined she did now. She closed her eyes. She had thought her tears had been expended before sleep last night. She chuckled lightly at herself. Who in her family would believe that the man she had so vehemently opposed in all things had now become the source of both her delight and sorrow?

It had been a delight to see him waiting for her under this very tree this morning. She had thought yesterday was the last she would see him until the month's end, but he refused to leave until he had seen her once more. So, while his coach and four sat on the side of the nearby road, he had come to stand under this tree until he had been able to give her the letter she now held. For a man of few words, his ability to write a letter and express his soul in those words was truly amazing. She lifted the paper that held his professions of love and longing to her lips and gave it a kiss. "And I love you, Fitzwilliam," she whispered before tucking the new letter into her pocket next to the old one. With one more deep sigh, she felt ready to continue her walk and face the day.

Jane and the Gardiners would be arriving the day after tomorrow. She must think on that. She rose, shook any bits of dirt or leaves from her skirts, squared her shoulders, and, affixing a smile to her lips, began walking in the direction of Willow Hall. Several times while she walked she had to remind herself to smile, to hide the pain that was in her heart, and every time she did, she wondered anew at how Jane was able to smile so very much.

"Ah, there you are," called Mrs. Abbot when Elizabeth neared the house. "I was afraid you might have gotten lost on your rambling." She tilted her head to the side and gave Elizabeth a searching look. "You look a bit worse for the wear this morning. Are you well?"

Elizabeth nodded. "I am well, although I must admit to not having slept soundly last night."

"Then you must take a rest after you have had your breakfast." She took Elizabeth by the arm and walked toward the house with her. "I dare say, with Mr. Darcy being gone, we will have fewer visitors today."

"I believe you are correct," said Elizabeth, the thought doing nothing to aid her in her attempts to smile and be pleasant. "However, the house will be full soon."

Mrs. Abbot squeezed Elizabeth's arm. "I am quite excited," she admitted. "I have not seen Marjorie in nearly a year. She was with me for Aiden's birth, you know."

Elizabeth nodded and allowed Cecily to prattle on about how delightful her younger son was and how he had nearly taken a step yesterday, which was at least a full month ahead of when his brother, Lucas, had attempted such a feat. The Abbot brothers were delightful. Elizabeth had spent many hours of her stay with them, reading books and building blocks, just as she had done with Aunt Gardiner's children when they were young.

"One day," Cecily was saying, "you will have your own children to crow about." She sat a cup of tea before Elizabeth. "Will it be soon?" she asked with a sly smile.

"I do not see how it can be," said Elizabeth with surprise. "It is still the practice to marry before having children, and I am not married."

Cecily laughed heartily at the comment. Gathering herself, she clarified, "I apologize for being unclear. I had meant will you be marrying soon, so that our little ones might grow up together?"

Elizabeth took a sip of her tea and slowly lowered the cup back to the table as she sought for a way to answer such a question without saying too much. She and Mr. Darcy had agreed that their understanding was to be of a secretive nature until he had been able to secure her father's approval. "I cannot say." Her cheeks glowed rosy. It was not a lie. She could not say without breaking her promise to Mr. Darcy, and yet, her heart felt it a half-truth.

A smile spread across Cecily's face. "Then, I

shall not press you on the matter until Mr. Darcy returns." The words were spoken in a loud whisper.

"Thank you," said Elizabeth. "I simply cannot say," she repeated.

Cecily patted her hand. "But it is not that you do not know."

Elizabeth's cheeks felt as if they were on fire now.

"I will say no more." Cecily pretended to lock her lips and place a key into her pocket.

Elizabeth rolled her eyes and shook her head.

"A fortnight is not so very long," Cecily commented as she lifted her own cup of tea and gave Elizabeth a wink. "He will be returned before you know it. I remember when my Harry would be gone for some reason or another — all related to business, of course."

Again, Elizabeth smiled and nodded and continued on with her breakfast while her friend told her story after story of the year before she and her husband were married and a bit about the year following.

"He was such a diligent worker. I am sure there is not another like him in all of Derbyshire." She paused to sip her tea. "And the Lord has rewarded us for it. Willow Hall is beautiful. My children are strong and healthy, and my Harry is no longer called away as he once was." She took another sip of tea. "He is still a hard worker. The best of men is what he is." She finished her tea. "Now look at me, talking and talking about my blessings and not allowing you a word."

"I enjoy hearing of your blessings, Cecily," assured Elizabeth. Indeed, it was what she had needed to take her mind off the events of the morning.

"Well, now," said Cecily after scrutinizing Elizabeth's face. "I must say you look better for having eaten." She stood. "Time for a rest."

Elizabeth sighed.

"No, I will not stand for you wearing yourself out and becoming ill." Cecily's hands were placed firmly on her hips, and although she was not more than six years Elizabeth's senior, she looked for all the world like a well-practiced matron. "One hour," she said definitively. "We shall not have visitors for at least one hour, so you are to lie on your bed until that time has passed."

Elizabeth rose to do as instructed but instead of allowing Elizabeth to pass, Cecily stepped in front of her and drew her into a firm embrace. "He will return like the wind. It was in his eyes," she whispered. Then, she gave Elizabeth a kiss on the cheek and allowed her to continue on her way.

Chapter 5

An hour is an incredibly small amount of time to lie on one's bed if weary, but when one's mind is filled with thoughts such as Elizabeth's was, it can be a very long time indeed. Feeling no more rested now than when she had first lain down, Elizabeth rose and readied herself for the possibility of callers.

"Oh, my, this is excellent news!" Cecily's voice carried from the sitting room and climbed the stairs to where Elizabeth was descending.

"Elizabeth! Elizabeth!" she called as she hurried into the hall. "Oh, Elizabeth, you will never guess, but it is the most excellent news." Cecily waved the letter she held. "Our sisters will be here tomorrow."

"Tomorrow?" Elizabeth said in surprise.

Cecily's head bobbed up and down, her smile

seeming to grow with each bob. "My brother Edward concluded his business early, and so they will arrive early." She clasped the letter to her chest. "Oh, I must alert Mrs. Smith. There is so much to be done."

"I dare say there is little to be done," said Harold Abbot as he watched his wife hurrying down the hall in search of the housekeeper.

Elizabeth laughed. "Very little needs doing. The beds have been made for three days now, and the rooms have been aired. I suppose it is just a matter of informing the cook of a larger number of guests for meals."

"And cutting fresh flowers," said Mr. Abbot.

Elizabeth sank into a chair in the sitting room and placed her workbasket on the floor next to her chair. She pulled out a piece that she had begun last week and prepared to work on it. "I suppose the flowers will be best gathered in the morning," she said.

Mr. Abbot agreed but worried slightly that his excited wife would not be able to wait so long to prepare. "I say, you do not seem so excited to see Jane as Cecily is to see Marjorie," he commented with a laugh.

"It has not been a year since I last saw Jane," explained Elizabeth.

Mr. Abbot smiled at her as he opened his book. "I dare say you would not be so exuberant as Cecily even if it had been a year. We each express our delight in different ways. Cecily happens to be more demonstrative than most, although not improperly so. Had we had company — beyond family — when the letter arrived, I know her excitement would have been better contained. However, I cannot fault her for her exuberance. It is a wonderful thing to have people you love visit after a long absence."

"Indeed," said Elizabeth. "I cannot imagine having so long a time away from Jane."

Mr. Abbot peeked up from his book and winked at her. "A hazard of marrying someone who is not local. But Edward is a good man and has done well for himself. It was a good match." He chuckled. "Not that I was even courting Cecily when Edward stole Marjorie away from Lambton." He lifted his book to read once again. "It would be nice to have more family settle in the area," he muttered.

He had not lifted the book quite high enough to hide the knowing smile that accompanied the statement, and Elizabeth was positive that it was done purposefully. The Abbots were so happy in their marriage that any news that hinted at another possible happy match always brought out their teasing natures.

Elizabeth shook her head and applied herself to her work, allowing the comment to go unanswered. She knew that neither Cecily or Harold would be indiscreet or excessive in their comments. She would merely have to endure a few remarks made in private and intended to let her know of their understanding and support.

It was a far cry better than what she would experience at home once her betrothal was made known. Her mother was not discreet, nor did she know how best to express her delight.

Elizabeth closed her eyes for a moment and sent a silent prayer toward heaven that her father would not tell her mother of the betrothal until after Mr. Darcy left. She knew Mr. Darcy was willing to accept her despite her mother, but there really was no need to make the acceptance more difficult than it needed to be.

As she stitched, her thoughts wandered from her mother, who was certain to be excessively excited, to her younger sisters, who were equally as likely to cause embarrassment. She sighed. At least Lydia was not at home. There might be some hope of Mary and Kitty behaving appropriately. So her thoughts continued for some time, and she was just beginning to think they would have a very quiet afternoon when the crunch of carriage wheels on the gravel of the drive wafted through the open window.

"At last," said Mr. Abbot, snapping his book closed. "I was afraid I was going to have to read for an entire afternoon." He winked again at Elizabeth, who smiled in return. Mr. Abbot was almost as fond of reading as her father or Uncle Gardiner. To have to pass an afternoon or evening with only a book as company would have been a very small hardship.

"It looks like Mr. Dobney," he said as he peered through the window. "He appears to have his sister and some other gentleman with him." He cocked his head to the side. "I do not think I have met him."

Elizabeth joined Mr. Abbot at the window to catch a glimpse of the stranger.

"Not a bad looking fellow," muttered Mr. Abbot.

Elizabeth had to agree. The gentleman seated next to Mr. Dobney was handsome. "But looks do not signify character," she added to her agreement.

"Quite so," Mr. Abbot agreed as they moved away from the window and took their seats once again until the party was announced and they rose in greeting.

"May I present my cousin, Captain Harris," said Marcus. "He arrived quite unexpectedly last evening."

Elizabeth noted the pointed look that Marcus gave to the man beside him.

"I promise I had written of my intent to call on my cousins," Captain Harris defended himself. "In fact, the letter arrived this morning."

"His directions were so poorly written," said Mary Ellen, "that it is a wonder we received it at all." She smiled at her cousin and spoke with a teasing tone. "But we did." She took a seat on the couch near Elizabeth and Captain Harris joined her once all the proper introductions had been made.

"You are in the militia?" Elizabeth queried.

Captain Harris gave a sharp nod of his head. "I am, but I have been given some time to visit family.

However, it will not be so long as it could be since the distance between Brighton and Derbyshire is not small."

"You are in Brighton?" Elizabeth asked with surprise. "You are not part of Colonel Forester's unit, are you?"

"No." Captain Harris shook his head firmly. "Colonel Fitzwilliam's." He tapped Mary Ellen's knee lightly with his own, causing her cheeks to flush.

"Mr. Darcy's cousin?"

"You know him?" asked Captain Harris.

Elizabeth nodded. "I met him in Kent at Easter. He is very pleasant, but I did not see him as a colonel, only as a guest of his aunt, so your opinion of him might be very different from mine, Captain Harris."

Captain Harris smiled. "I hold my colonel in highest regard, Miss Bennet. He is among the best."

"It is good to hear my judgement of him was not mistaken." Elizabeth was sure it sounded like the correct thing to say, but to her, whose judgement had been so very flawed regarding so many people, it was much more than a comment to be thrown away. It was an acknowledgement that she was not totally without sense in judging character.

"Now, Colonel Forester has the marking of one day being a fine colonel, but..." He shook his head and clucked his tongue softly, "he has been given quite the challenging band of recruits. A rather ragtag and bobtail lot they are."

Elizabeth's brows rose in surprise. She had not thought the regiment from Meryton was so very bad.

"Oh, not the whole lot, that is very unfair of me to say." Seeing her expression, he adjusted his estimation. "It seems it is always just a few who make the reputation of the whole."

She could not disagree with that, although she felt as if she should, for his judgement seemed presumptuous. Colonel Forester had been a very agreeable man, and she knew that he did not use discipline sparingly. "Do Colonel Forester and his wife get on well?"

The question was asked but remained unanswered for some minutes as Cecily finally returned to the room just before the tea tray, requiring that introductions be made. Finally, when tea had been served, Captain Harris returned to their discussion.

"I do not wish to offend," he said softly, "but Mrs. Forester is a bit silly, although I am certain that much of that has to do with her age. She is not very old." He took a sip of his tea. "She has a friend staying with her. A bit of a flirt." He took another sip of his tea. "Oh, what is her name? I should know it. I am sure I have heard it in a half dozen or so conversations."

Elizabeth sighed. "Miss Bennet."

Captain Harris grimaced. "A relation?" he asked.

"My sister."

"Well, I have put my foot in it now, haven't I?" He shook his head and smiled sheepishly.

Although Elizabeth was indeed mortified to hear a complete stranger refer to her sister as a flirt, she was glad to hear something of how Lydia fared. Jane had shared some of what Lydia had written to Kitty, but it was all uniforms, handsome men, and soirees with a bit about the sites and sea at Brighton.

"I would rather the truth than a pleasing lie," said Elizabeth with a smile. "I am sorry to say that my youngest sister is an incurable flirt. Please tell me that she has not done anything to bring utter shame to her family." She held up a finger. "But only if it is the truth. I shall prepare myself for the worst, of course."

"She is a trial to you?" asked Mary Ellen.

"She acts without thought," Elizabeth said quietly. "She has a lively spirit, but it has been left unchecked." Her cheeks burned with the admission that her father had not done his duty by his family through allowing Lydia to continue as she always had.

"That is unfortunate." Mary Ellen placed a hand on Elizabeth's.

Elizabeth nodded her agreement.

"I assure you," said Captain Harris, "that beyond flirting, I have not heard of anything improper." He grimaced once again. "However, the objects of her flirtation leave something to be desired."

Elizabeth shook her head and closed her eyes. She knew of whom he spoke. "Mr. Wickham is still among that number?" To her surprise, she felt Mary Ellen's hand tighten on hers. The action made the small nervous fluttering sensation in her stomach, which she felt each time she thought of Lydia in Brighton, grow to a churning. The look of concern in Mary Ellen's eyes when Elizabeth looked at her did nothing to quell the nerves.

"He is." Captain Harris' voice was grave. "He is not a proper companion for any young lady."

Elizabeth sighed. She knew this to be true now. How she longed to go back to last fall and reform her impressions of him then. Perhaps, if she had taken a more careful look at what Mr. Wickham said and how he presented himself, she might have saved her family and Lydia the association. But, she had not, and now she must bear the weight of that error. "I know," she replied softly.

Captain Harris's smile was sympathetic. "I fear he missed his calling by joining the militia. He is far better suited to the stage, for he certainly knows how to play a part."

Elizabeth nodded. "That I also know."

"As do many," said Mary Ellen. "He is quite convincing." She turned to her cousin. "Perhaps it should be suggested to him. I am certain the fame and fawning which would accompany such a profession would be very appealing to him. A letter to Colonel Fitzwilliam, perhaps?" She spoke lightly as if teasing, but her eyes were serious.

Captain Harris' brows furrowed for a moment

before he chuckled. "I shall make mention of it to him; however, I shall have to do so soon, as he is set to depart Brighton for town and then Derbyshire in a week's time. I am not sure a post would reach him in time. "

"Oh," said Mary Ellen with a wave of her hand, "we shall send it express, and I shall write the directions so that it will not get lost." She giggled softly as if it were a great joke, but Elizabeth noted how Mary Ellen's grasp on her hand had not yet loosened. It was obvious that the young woman was more fearful than she allowed in her comments. Perhaps she knew of Georgiana's ordeal. She was friends with both Mr. Darcy and his sister.

"Colonel Fitzwilliam is to come to Derbyshire?" Elizabeth asked.

"Aye, he is planning to visit his cousins and his parents, of course. Lord and Lady Matlock have retired to their estate for the summer. I am to remain here until he is to return. Then I am to accompany him, as his current escorts will be given a few weeks to visit their families. Our unit, you see, originates from the towns around here." He tipped his head and peered at Elizabeth, whose brows were furrowed quite deeply as she thought. "Is there something troubling you, Miss Bennet?"

"I was merely wondering why, if Mr. Wickham is from Derbyshire, he is in Colonel Forester's unit and not yours."

"His home is now in London." Mary Ellen's comment was quick.

"Oh," said Elizabeth softly. From the sharpness of her companion's reply, she was fearful that she had offended but did not know how or why.

Mary Ellen, finally, released Elizabeth's hand and gave it a reassuring pat. "He is no longer welcome here," she said softly. "I dare not say more, for it is not my tale to tell." She bit her lip and studied Elizabeth's face.

"Very well," she said after a moment, "I should not say, but since your sister is well within his sphere of influence, you may wish to speak to Lucy regarding Mr. Wickham, but, please, when you do, be gentle. It is not a pleasant tale."

Elizabeth's heart sank. Lucy, too? How many people had this man injured? Her spirit was troubled for the remainder of the visit and well into the evening. No matter how many times Cecily managed to speak of the arrival of Mrs.

Gardiner and Jane, Elizabeth's spirit would not be lifted for more than a few moments.

Finally, as she prepared for bed, she determined that tomorrow, before Jane arrived, she would call on Mrs. Dobney. It was better, she supposed, to hear the sordid tale than to imagine what it might be. Then, she would also be better able to decide if she should write to her father. Perhaps if he knew details of the character of some of the men at Brighton, he would see reason and have Lydia returned home before anything irreversible could happen. Plan in place, she blew out her candle and snuggled under the covers.

Chapter 6

Elizabeth stood just beyond a low border, watching Cecily play with her children in the garden. The ball rolled toward the large tree that shadowed the far corner, and Lucas Abbot, the elder brother at nearly four years of age, ran after it while Aiden Abbott, the younger brother and just three months past his first birthday, swayed slightly and then took one wobbly step followed by another equally unstable step before falling with a plop to the ground. The action of dropping so ungracefully to the ground did not please the young child. His scowl before he took to crawling after his brother made Elizabeth smile. He was a determined young man. A little fall was not going to stop him from pursuing his goal, which at this moment was the ball with which his brother was taunting him.

Cecily waved to Elizabeth. "Come, join us."

Elizabeth, having just returned from what had proven to be a rather disturbing call at the parsonage and wishing for some time to think about all Lucy had shared with her, would have made her excuses and gone into the house. However, the motion of his mother had turned Aiden toward Elizabeth, and the ball was seemingly forgotten in favour of the new arrival.

"Izabef!" Lucas, ball in hand, reached her before his brother could. "Will you play ball with me, Izabef?"

Elizabeth tousled the boy's hair. "Of course. Do you wish to run before I throw it?"

The young man's head shook furiously from side to side. "I want to race it."

"Very well." Elizabeth took the ball from his hands and squatted down. "Ready," she warned. "Go."

The ball rolled along the grass, passing just beside Aiden, who stopped and sat, looking first at Elizabeth and then the ball — clearly unsure which should get his attention.

"Aiden," Elizabeth called. "Come." She bent down and held out her hands toward him. The smile he turned on her would have been enough of a reward in itself, but the feeling of chubby little arms encircling her neck and a head nuzzling into her shoulder was even better.

"You are a natural," said Cecily as she took Elizabeth's arm and led her to a bench not far from the tree at the end of the garden.

Shadows of shade danced across the bench as the breeze rustled the leaves of the less mature tree beside it. Lucas had returned with his ball, wishing for it to be tossed once again. Cecily obliged him.

"It is his favourite game. He can roll it himself, of course, but he prefers running after it when someone else has rolled it. See how he tries to reach the tree before the ball?"

"I do. He is very quick."

Elizabeth sat Aiden on her lap and squeezed him tightly. He snuggled into her arms and stayed there peacefully for a moment until Lucas once again returned. Then, with a babble that sounded like ball, he began twisting and turning to free himself.

"Very well, young man." Elizabeth stood him on his feet. He teetered a bit, but this time he managed three steps before landing on the ground. "He will be chasing after Lucas before long."

"That he will," said Cecily proudly. "They do

keep their nurse busy. When I looked in on them this afternoon, she looked as if she could use a few quiet moments, and I could not resist the beautiful weather. So, here we are. My duties are complete for the moment, and I am free to enjoy the garden with my dear boys. It is one of the great pleasures of motherhood."

Elizabeth closed her eyes and drew a deep breath. "It is a lovely day," she agreed. "I would also choose to sit in the garden on a day like today if I could not take a walk."

"Your walk was pleasant?" It was more than a pleasantry. Elizabeth could hear the curiosity that lay behind the nonchalance of the comment.

"It was." Elizabeth's smile was teasing. She knew what information Cecily sought. "Not a cloud in the sky. A soft breeze to cool me, and a few birds to add their choruses to my reverie."

"And Mrs. Dobney is well?"

Elizabeth nodded. "Quite well, as is Mr. Dobney."

Cecily sighed. "Are you going to make me ask?"

Elizabeth giggled at the exasperated look on Cecily's face.

"Very well," said Cecily, "was your talk enlightening?"

"Very." Elizabeth assisted the child who was tugging at her skirt to stand. "I must write to my father. Mr. Wickham's character is..." She searched for the best word to describe him. "Reprehensible, completely, utterly reprehensible."

"I have heard enough to agree." Cecily rolled Lucas' ball and, as he scampered after it, turned toward Elizabeth. "I shall not ask you the details, though you know the suffering I must endure not to do so." She laughed as she pulled herself straight and primly folded her hands in her lap. "I will not be like my mother. I absolutely refuse to be a tattler like she. It is not right, no matter how tantalizing and delicious the topic." She sighed, her spine curving as if under a great weight. "Doing right is often very hard."

Elizabeth wrapped an arm around Cecily's shoulders. "It is." She squeezed her friend closely. "I only wish I had done what was right and not listened to Mr. Wickham's tales."

Cecily snaked an arm around Elizabeth's waist and returned the squeeze. "Regret touches us all at one time or another. The trick is to seek forgiveness and proceed with greater wisdom."

She released Elizabeth from her embrace so that she could roll the ball one more time for Lucas. Then, she looked at Elizabeth. It was not a casual or playful glance. No, this was a look that spoke of the seriousness of the words to be spoken and of the love that the speaker had for the hearer.

"A mistake must be forgiven not only by the person wronged but also by the one who committed the error. I believe you have the forgiveness of the person injured." She smiled as Elizabeth nodded. "But do you have your own forgiveness?" She patted Elizabeth's knee.

"Come. We must return these young gentlemen to their nurse so that we might have a few moments of rest before our sisters arrive." She stood and looked over her shoulder at Elizabeth. "I shall catch Lucas if you will take Aiden." She waited for no reply but called to her eldest and dashed toward the tree.

Lucas squealed and darted behind the tree where he stood peeking around it looking for his mother. Elizabeth laughed at the increased squealing and giggling that came from the child as his mother grabbed him and swung him about in a circle before instructing him to get his ball and follow her.

"You heard your mama," Elizabeth said to Aiden. "It is time to return to the nursery." She took hold of each of his pudgy little hands and hoisted him to his feet, allowing him to walk a short distance before snatching him up and carrying him the rest of the way.

~*~*~

Lucy pushed the door to Philip's study open slowly, peeking around it to see if she would be disturbing him. He glanced up from the book he was reading and smiled. Taking that as his welcome, she slipped into the room.

"You had a visitor this morning?" Philip placed the book to the side and leaned forward, resting his elbows on the desk as he crossed his arms.

"I did." Lucy arranged her skirts around her legs. She and Elizabeth had spoken in confidence, but after a time of consideration, she had decided that it was better to share what had been said with her husband than to keep it to herself. Philip was not one to tell tales, and he was a good friend of Darcy's.

"We spoke of Wickham." She knew it was not exactly the softest way to begin this conversation, but then, why try to speak softly of a man such as Wickham? Philip knew as well as she did the sort of man Wickham was. "And my uncle," she added.

Philip's eyes grew wide.

"Your cousin has arrived, and he and Mary Ellen called on the Abbots."

Philip's brows furrowed as he attempted to piece together the puzzle of information his wife was presenting.

"It seems Wickham is in the militia."

Philip nodded slowly. Now it was beginning to make a modicum of sense.

"His unit was stationed for the fall and winter in Hertfordshire."

Philip nodded again. "I believe one of Darcy's letters mentioned having seen the man."

"He befriended Miss Elizabeth."

Philip expelled a slow breath. Not only was the reason for Miss Elizabeth's visit becoming understandable, but several comments from Darcy's letters were also gaining clarity. "He told her lies about Darcy."

Lucy nodded. "And she believed him. She feels

dreadful about having done so." She peeked up at her husband. "Darcy has forgiven her, of course." She considered telling him about Elizabeth's tale of Darcy's failed proposal and the letter he had written her but decided it was not necessary as Philip quite likely already knew of those details. And from the look of understanding on his face, she guessed that her theory was correct.

"That is not the reason she wished to speak of Wickham, however. As you know, Miss Elizabeth has several sisters."

Her husband nodded his agreement.

"The youngest, Miss Lydia, is sixteen and quite taken with Wickham." When she had heard it from Elizabeth, Lucy had felt as if someone has tried to steal her breath, and she saw that same look on her husband's face. "Miss Lydia has gone to Brighton with her particular friend, who happens to be the wife of the colonel in charge of Wickham."

Philip sank back into his chair and shook his head. "Who would send one so young to such a place as Brighton?"

"Miss Elizabeth said she tried to convince her father that it was not a good idea, but she could not give him her full reasoning as she did not wish to betray a confidence."

"She knows of Georgiana?"

Lucy nodded. "She does, and your cousin has made her aware of a continued flirtation between Miss Lydia and Wickham." She drew a deep breath and expelled it. "I have given her permission to mention some of what happened to me to her father. She will not name me but will provide general details of what she has heard of Wickham. She is hopeful that in so doing, her father might find it necessary to have Miss Lydia returned to Hertfordshire."

They sat quietly for a while — Philip drumming his fingers on the desk as he thought and Lucy watching him. Finally, Philip rose from his chair. "I believe we must visit my cousin, my dear. I am surprised he has not come to call already."

He came around to the front of the desk and extended his arm to Lucy. "And then, I must write Darcy a letter informing him of Captain Harris' arrival."

"You must?" Lucy asked in surprise.

Philip chuckled. "I promised I would write if any new gentlemen arrived in the area — not that I fear my cousin will persuade Miss Elizabeth away from Darcy. However, I should not like to be on the receiving end of Darcy's displeasure should he hear that Harris is here, and I did not inform him."

Lucy laughed. "I doubt there is anyone who could steal Miss Elizabeth away from Darcy."

"Yes," agreed Philip, "but having almost lost her once, he is unwilling to take the risk once again."

Lucy collected her bonnet from the table in the entry as Philip requested his curricle made ready. "So, it is as I expected?"

He opened the door and allowed her to exit before him. "Indeed, if all goes well in Hertfordshire, we shall soon be adding Miss Elizabeth to our numbers here in Derbyshire." He looked down at his wife's beaming smile. "But," he cautioned as they stood waiting for the curricle to be brought around, "we are not to know."

Chapter 7

Hertfordshire

Mr. Bennet gave the gentleman who entered his study an inquisitive look. "It is a surprise to see you, Mr. Darcy." He motioned for him to take a seat. "Is this a social call?"

Darcy did not miss the skeptical tone of Mr. Bennet's question.

"I am not fond of social calls," Darcy admitted knowing that such a comment was bound to earn him a chuckle at his own expense — which it did.

"I find them tedious myself," Mr. Bennet replied. "So if it is not social, I must assume we have some business to discuss, although I cannot say I have any inkling as to what business we might have."

"I have been in Derbyshire," Darcy began.

"You have seen my Lizzy? Does she send news?"

"I have, and she does." He took the letter

Elizabeth had written to her father out of his pocket and handed it to Mr. Bennet.

"You could have left it with Hill." Mr. Bennet took the letter. "Were you instructed to await a reply?"

"I was not instructed," said Darcy, "but I will need a reply."

A look of skepticism mixed with intrigue crept across Mr. Bennet's face. "Elizabeth has been in Derbyshire for some weeks now. Have you been there with her that whole time?"

Darcy wished the man would just open the letter instead of plying him with questions. "No, just the past week and not even all of that. I was in town but travelled home to accompany my sister on her return there and to check on my tenants at Willow Hall."

"Willow Hall is yours?"

"I purchased it last year before I travelled to Netherfield with Bingley."

Mr. Bennet nodded and looked thoughtful. "So Sir William was not exaggerating when he said you owned half of Derbyshire?"

"I would not say half, but I do own a significant portion," Darcy admitted.

"Sir William can get carried away," explained Mr. Bennet. "The sky is always sunnier than it truly is, so to speak. He is a very pleasant sort of fellow and a true friend with a kind heart, but his version of reality is always slightly better than it is, or so I find." He turned the letter over in his hand. "I assume you wish me to read this before you divulge your reason for being here."

"I thought it best to let your daughter have her say first."

Mr. Bennet's lips twitched. "A wise man," he said as he broke the seal.

Darcy chewed the inside of his cheek while Mr. Bennet opened the letter that Elizabeth had sent. Breathing had never felt like such a task before this moment. Darcy's fingers itched to loosen his cravat, but, with no small amount of effort, he held them still in his lap except for one thumb that tapped against the inside of his knee.

Mr. Bennet pushed his round spectacles up the bridge of his nose slightly before turning his attention to what his daughter had written.

Darcy knew what it said, for Elizabeth had shown it to him — not that he had asked to see it. No, he would have delivered it without knowing an ounce of its contents, but Elizabeth was determined that there be no secrets between them. He shifted slightly in his chair as Mr. Bennet made a slightly startled, chuckling sound. Finally, the gentleman placed the letter on his desk, removed his spectacles, and leaning back in his chair, studied Darcy.

If having to wait for the man to read the contents of the letter was uncomfortable, being the object of that man's scrutiny for a period of several minutes was nigh unto torture. Darcy wished to have the ordeal over, but he would not speak first.

At length, Mr. Bennet leaned forward once again, replaced his spectacles, and picked up the letter for a second perusal. "It seems, Mr. Darcy, that my daughter has taken a liking to you after all."

"She has, sir."

"She is not one to change her opinion of a person once it has been firmly made," he peeked up at Darcy, "unless she has been proven wrong, and the evidence would have to be nearly irrefutable. She is nearly as stubborn as her mother."

He chuckled. "Do not worry, Mr. Darcy, she has far more sense than her mother. Your life should be decorated with fewer flutters of nerves than mine ever has been." He placed the letter on the desk. "I suppose we should consider the particulars of the arrangement, but I will not deny my daughter her wish so long as the details are agreeable. So," he waggled his eyebrows as he placed his spectacles on the desk next to the letter, "you may breathe now. I really am not so formidable."

He sighed as a raised voice and a slamming door were heard above them. "If I were, I am sure my house would be more serene." He settled back in his chair, propped his elbows on the arms of the chair, and tucked his fingers into the small pockets on his waistcoat. "I do suppose I should do the proper thing and hear your reasons for wishing to marry my daughter and into this family." His eyes narrowed slightly and his tone was serious as he said the last few words.

"There is only one reason, sir. I love your daughter and always shall." He felt the flush that such admissions might necessarily bring creep up his neck and warm his ears. "I know that my behaviour when I was last in Hertfordshire was not what it should have been. I was dour and disagreeable. I said things that were both unpleasant and untrue. Neither my words nor my actions were gentlemanly, and I must apologize." He held Mr. Bennet's gaze. "They cost me dearly." He swallowed and drew a breath before continuing. "Your daughter refused my first proposal of marriage."

"First?" Shock suffused Mr. Bennet's face.

"Yes, sir. I offered her my heart and my hand when she was visiting her cousin in Kent." He smiled wryly and shook his head. "I assure you I was most handily and heartily chastised for my prior behaviour."

Mr. Bennet chuckled at the admission. "She has a sharp tongue and a temper, that, although it is not quick, it is fearsome."

"That she does," Darcy admitted. How her words had cut him and flared his own indignation! "Her anger was not unjust."

"It will be part of what she brings to your marriage," Mr. Bennet cautioned.

Darcy nodded. "Of that I am aware, but I believe we have come to understand each other better since that day, and such knowledge might save me from earning her displeasure too often."

Again, Mr. Bennet chuckled. "So you are wise enough to know that yours will not be a marriage without argument?"

"I hope I am."

"Very good." He cocked his head to the side and studied Darcy once again. "Perhaps I should hear the facts that swayed my daughter to alter her opinion of you."

"You will not withdraw your consent?"

"My Lizzy is no fool, Mr. Darcy. If she finds good in you despite whatever it is that you are reluctant to share, then there is good in you. My consent shall stand." His eyes twinkled. "However, if it is of a very distressful nature, I may require you to stay for dinner with my wife and daughters."

Darcy grimaced as he knew that what he had to say was not flattering. "You might wish to inform your cook there will be an extra plate at dinner."

Mr. Bennet's brows rose.

"I was not lying when I said I behaved poorly," explained Darcy. "There were several charges laid at my feet by your daughter. One of those charges has to do with my friend."

"Ah, so you did separate them." Mr. Bennet's

lips were set in a firm line, and his eyes lacked any merriment.

At such a response that confirmed what Elizabeth had said of Jane's despondence, Darcy felt the guilt he had carried over such actions grow. He would not be pleased with anyone that caused such heartache for his sister. Nor, if he had several sisters or daughters to see well-situated, would he willingly forgive that person for possibly dashing the possibility of a good match. He hoped that Mr. Bennet would be less reticent.

"I did. I had not observed a strong attachment on Miss Bennet's part, but I had seen enough to know that my friend's heart was in grave danger of being seriously injured if she did not return his admiration."

Mr. Bennet sat quietly for a moment before saying, "Yes, yes, Jane is far too calm for her own good. I wish she had just an ounce more of Lizzy's pluck." He shook his head. "It is not a flattering admission, but not being of the female gender, I find I can understand the decision better than my Lizzy would. She and Jane are quite attached, as I am sure you are aware."

"I am," Darcy admitted. He drew another deep

breath. Confessing to one's follies was not easily done. "At Easter, when I proposed to Miss Elizabeth in Kent, I explained my feelings to her by telling her about the many obstacles I had to overcome before I could follow where my heart led."

Amusement played at Mr. Bennet's mouth. "She does not have the connections a family such as yours would welcome."

"Indeed."

"That was badly done," muttered Mr. Bennet.

"Indeed," repeated Darcy. "I am ashamed to say that I spoke ill of your family." Again, as a shadow of sadness passed over Mr. Bennet's face, Darcy felt the shame of his words deepen in his chest. "It was wrong. My family is not without fault and to hold others to a standard that my family does not even meet was pure arrogance."

"Is that all?" Mr. Bennet asked.

Darcy shook his head. "I wish it were, but it is not. However, before I relate the rest, I must have your assurance of secrecy as part of the tale involves both a friend and my sister. I have told Miss Elizabeth the portion of the tale as it relates to my sister, but not the part about Miss Tolson. I had not thought to tell her about that, but I understand your youngest daughter has gone to Brighton."

Mr. Bennet's brows furrowed. "Of course, I will say nothing." He stood and crossed behind his desk to the side of the room away from the windows. He lifted a decanter of port and with his eyes and a tip of his head inquired if Darcy would like a bit.

"Please," Darcy accepted. He always found it easier to speak of Wickham when there was something to warm his throat and push down the bile that arose. How close he had come to losing his sister! No matter what counsel he gave himself or received from a friend, he could not discuss the story without feeling his failure — even now, a year after the incident.

Mr. Bennet refilled his glass twice over and Darcy's once during the recital of events leading to Darcy's purchase of Willow Hall to protect Lucy from her uncle and Wickham's scheming. Then, as both men cradled empty glasses in their hands, Darcy shared about Georgiana's near elopement.

Mr. Bennet tipped his glass this way and that, catching a bit of afternoon sunlight with one of the cut-out designs and separating the light into a rainbow of colours. "You have given me much about which to think." He placed his glass on the desk. "However, that will have to wait. I believe, we have a marriage agreement to discuss." He pulled out paper and pen for making notes. "You will, of course, be required to stand by my side when I tell my wife. That should bring us to even. You have spoken ill of my Lizzy and my family — not all unjustly, I am certain — but there must be some recompense." He chuckled. "It will be like nothing you have ever witnessed before, I can assure you of that."

Darcy did not quite catch the grimace that accompanied such news. This made Mr. Bennet chortle even more as he dipped his pen in the ink. "Shall we start with what Elizabeth will bring to the marriage — other than her mother."

~*~*~

Darcy was, of course, also subjected to supper with Mrs. Bennet and her daughters as he had suspected he would be. Whether it was as additional penance for his previously poor behaviour or as a means to gain Mr. Bennet a conversation partner, he was not certain.

After their meal, he made his excuses and

attempted to leave, but Mrs. Bennet was not to be moved from the fact that travel at such an hour was entirely unwise. And so, after a time of entertainment and chatter, much of which he only marginally enjoyed, Darcy found himself tucked into the guest room at Longbourn. It was small but tidy and welcoming.

A footman was dispatched to attend him, and then, with a borrowed book, he was left to himself. Propping a pillow behind his back and tucking the blankets about his legs, he made ready to read a few lines of poetry before attempting sleep. Down the hall, which was not so very long, he could hear the shuffling of furniture and closing of doors as the others prepared for sleep as well. A humming came from the same direction, grew louder as it passed, and faded as it disappeared, he supposed, behind the door that led to the servants' stairs.

He shook his head. How different this was from what he had become accustomed to! This was the noise which, to Elizabeth, was familiar. He considered his evening. Yes, it had been uncomfortable, but it was not due to the Bennets. No, it was due to his own inclinations for solitude. With a smile, he opened the book of poetry. He was certain he could get used to a bit of the noise associated with a family such as this.

A door opened down the hall, and there was the scurrying of feet and a good night was called from one sister to another. He grimaced slightly at the force with which the next door had been closed. Yes, he could get used to such noises, but it would take time, and he might need to take them in small doses, at first.

The book had fallen open to where it had been marked with a paper. Unfolding the paper, Darcy found a drawing entitled *What Walks We Take, What Books We Choose*. There was a rough form of a girl and her father walking along a path toward a rise in the distance. He held the picture closer to the candle and examined it carefully. The figures seemed to be carrying something, which he assumed from their square shape and the title, were books. He chuckled. It was obviously the work of a young hand. He continued to look at the picture for a moment. Finally, his eyes came to rest on the artist's signature.

To my Papa,
With all my love,
your Lizzy

With a smile, he folded the paper once again and tucked it back into the book and began to read. For a few moments he disciplined his mind to pay attention to the words that Mr. Cowper had penned, but eventually, his mind refused to cooperate, and taking one last look at a young Elizabeth's gift to her father, he set the book aside, blew out his candle and prepared to sleep.

Chapter 8

The next morning, Darcy was again assisted by the same footman who had helped him the night before.

"The master has requested you attend him in his study," the footman said as he helped Darcy into his boots and jacket. "He has had some tea and muffins made ready there."

Darcy thanked the man for the message and made his way to Mr. Bennet's study.

"Ah, there you are. I figured you for an early riser." He put down his pen and motioned to the tea on the corner of his desk. "I prefer a quiet cup in here before facing the rest of the house."

He took his cup and settled back in his chair. "On occasion, I am joined by Jane and Lizzy. Mary rises just as early, but she prefers to find a corner near the window in the drawing room, so that she can read before her mother finds her and sets her about her tasks for the day. I imagine, from the soft footsteps I heard just a few minutes before you arrived, that she is there now."

One eyebrow cocked as a smile played at his lips. "My wife and two youngest are not late risers by any means, but they are not early either."

He placed his cup on the desk. "You slept well?"

"I did, thank you."

"Very good. I did not." He sighed. "Lizzy warned me of the danger that sending Lydia away might pose, but I did not think it so bad a thing. Colonel Forester seemed a respectable sort of fellow, and he assured me he would hold her to the rules of propriety," he sighed again, "at least as far as a high-spirited young lady like Lydia can be held to them."

He picked up the paper that lay on the desk in front of him. "I am sending an express to Colonel Forester this morning and will depart today for Brighton to retrieve Lydia." He sighed for a third time. "It will not be a pleasant task, I assure you. Between the wailing that will occur before I have left my door to the wailing that will accompany me from the shore until I return –" He shook his head.

"It is no more than I deserve. I should have listened to reason, but I did not." He folded and sealed his letter.

"It seems a reasonable plan." Darcy was relieved that Mr. Bennet had come to the conclusion that action needed to be taken immediately. Even so, he still felt a small measure of trepidation that even with such swift action, it might be too late. But he knew also that other than riding through the night, the trip could not have happened any sooner. "Will you allow me to return your hospitality by spending the night at Darcy House?"

Mr. Bennet smiled sheepishly. "Gardiner has already departed for Derbyshire, so I had hoped you would offer," he admitted.

Darcy smiled at the admission and made one of his own. "My motives are not so pure as you might assume."

Mr. Bennet raised a questioning brow.

"I expect to see Bingley this evening."

Mr. Bennet laughed. "I shall stand by your side, but I'll not be your second."

Darcy laughed with him. He hoped that having Mr. Bennet there might soften the response he knew he faced — and rightly so — from his friend.

Bingley was amiable to a fault, but he was not without a temper. More than one chap at school had had an eye blackened or a lip split by Bingley, usually over some comment concerning his connections to trade and, often, followed by the comment,

"Ah, tradesmen, ruffians, the whole lot, is that not right?"

The injured would assuredly agree, which was as Bingley planned, so that he might then add,

"I should hate to have anyone think you a liar, so you may thank me for keeping your point valid."

All this Darcy shared with Mr. Bennet.

When Mr. Bennet had finally stopped chuckling over the information and had repeated *"thank me for keeping your point valid"* for the fourth time. He took a sip of tea and commented, "I hadn't thought him to be so quick with a quip."

"He is not, but occasionally, he will surprise you," said Darcy. "He is, however, quick with his hands, so if you would stand in front of me, I should feel much safer than if you stand beside me." Darcy smirked as Mr. Bennet raised his brows in surprise. "No need to fear, sir. Although I have become well-versed in the art of teasing through my cousin, Colonel Fitzwilliam, I do not engage in the activity very often. Often, the moment has passed before I have thought of a reply." He lifted a shoulder in a half-shrug. "My nature is more serious, I suppose."

Mr. Bennet chuckled again. "I doubt you will remain so serious for long."

Darcy returned Mr. Bennet's grin. "I am not opposed to change — at least not completely."

"Just not quick to make it?" Mr. Bennet raised a brow, peering over his cup, as he finished his tea.

"Guilty as charged," said Darcy with a small bow of his head. "However, when a change is for the better and a reasonable explanation has been given, the alteration is made posthaste."

"Nothing by halves, is it?"

"Very little."

"You and my daughter are very similar in that way." He stood, his sealed express in his hand. "I shall send this off and then inform my wife of my plans. You are welcome to take refuge in here for as long as you wish. Breakfast will be spread out in about a half hour's time, and we can leave quite soon after."

Darcy thanked him and poured a second cup of

tea. Then, selecting a book from one of the shelves, sat down to enjoy it and his beverage in relative peace as voices were heard above stairs and a servant or two scurried to answer.

~*~*~

Finally, when all the details necessary before a trip had been seen to, Darcy allowed Mr. Bennet to climb into the carriage and arrange himself comfortably before entering the coach and taking the seat opposite of the gentleman. They were just moving away from the front of Longbourn, and Mr. Bennet was complimenting Darcy on the fineness of the carriage when a rider entered the drive.

"What can that be?" asked Mr. Bennet as Darcy tapped on the roof to get the carriage to stop.

"Ho, there!" Darcy heard his coachman call to the rider. "The master be inside the carriage if ye be looking for him."

"Indeed, I am," returned the rider as he slowed his horse and swung off in a fluid motion, landing next to his mount as it stopped. "I've a message for 'im." The rider pulled a letter from his bag and approached the carriage as a footman opened the door. "Mr. Thomas Bennet?" The rider looked between the two gentlemen in the carriage.

"That would be me," said Mr. Bennet, accepting the letter and thanking the rider, who was gone nearly as quickly as he had appeared.

Darcy watched Mr. Bennet's eyes grow wide and his skin pale as he read the message. "Is something amiss?" he asked quietly.

Mr. Bennet replied by passing him the letter.

Sir,

I must inform you of some unfortunate news and my failure. Miss Lydia went out to the shops this morning with her maid, and neither has returned as of the time of my writing this letter. (It is now six o'clock.)

We have searched the area, to no avail. However, I have heard that she was seen boarding a mail coach bound for London. I wish this was the extent of my news, but I must inform you that the mail coach also carried three of my men, who are enjoying a period of time away from their duties. One of these men, Lieutenant Wickham, has paid particular attention to your daughter and she to him. It is rumoured that they do not intend to stop in London but continue on to Gretna Green. I have no evidence to support this claim save the departure of both, but I could not in good conscience omit that information whether substantiated or not. There are men already on their way to London to try to apprehend Miss Lydia before it is too late to do so.

I must humbly beg your forgiveness in this matter...

Darcy scanned the remaining few words of apology before handing the letter back to Mr. Bennet.

Mr. Bennet shook his head. "Had I listened to Lizzy," he muttered.

"Had I told you of Wickham earlier," said Darcy.

"Ah, we are a sorry pair, are we not? Sitting here regretting what cannot be undone." Mr. Bennet tucked the letter in his pocket. "I'll not make mention of this to my wife just yet. It would be best to see if we can find out anything once we get to town. However, if we might take a few moments for me to write a reply to Forrester and then have it posted at the first stop along the road?"

"Of course," said Darcy. "Time is of the essence."

"Indeed," agreed Mr. Bennet. "I shall be mere moments." He climbed down from the carriage as quickly as he could.

Darcy climbed out and stood next to his carriage, watching as Mr. Bennet met his wife, who was fluttering on about what the rider could have wanted. "Just some business that needs attention. Nothing to worry about at present, my dear," he said as he took her arm and wound it around his.

Darcy was glad when just a few moments had passed and Mr. Bennet once again appeared.

"All is well within," Mr. Bennet assured him. "None the wiser." He settled into his seat. "I do not like the idea of being away while she is in a state." He peered out the window toward the house. "But I spoke to Mary, and she will care for her."

The tone of the comment took Darcy by surprise. He had expected a less worried tone or perhaps a funny quip about nerves and females. But from the way the man looked back several more times, Darcy got the feeling that though the man across from him may not act the part of a smitten husband or a doting papa, he was far from the unconcerned husband he portrayed.

Once Longbourn was well behind them, they traded a few pleasantries and then each indulged himself in a book. It was a quiet trip, but not uncomfortably so. It seems that each man respected the need of the other for solitude. There were a few moments of friendly discussion at each stop and occasionally as something came to the mind of Mr. Bennet that he felt needed to be pondered, but aside from those few and well-dispersed interactions, the remainder of the trip was silent within the carriage, save for the shifting for comfort in seats and the turning of pages.

Mr. Bennet closed his book and placed it on the seat next to him. "I do not know where to begin," he said looking out the window toward the city that was before them.

Darcy also closed his book. He could well imagine the concern that ran through Mr. Bennet's mind. "I may know of a few places to check if Wickham still associates with the men he once did." He smiled ruefully. "They are not pleasant places, so I will send someone to inquire before venturing out myself. That should also make the search swifter."

Mr. Bennet nodded thoughtfully. "I admit I know little of London besides Cheapside and Gracechurch Street. I leave the exploration of shops to the ladies." He chuckled lightly. "Aside from the occasional foray into a bookshop."

"You shall have to allow me to show you the sites on some visit." The carriage was winding its way through the streets. "I imagine the museum would be of interest to you?" He nearly laughed as the gentleman's eyes could not hide his delight at such a thought. "But for tonight you may have to content yourself with my library."

This, of course, prompted one of the longest discussions of their journey as Mr. Bennet inquired about particular authors and books, and Darcy delighted in telling him of all he asked plus a few of his prize acquisitions.

"I believe you shall be my favourite son," declared Mr. Bennet. "And to think I thought it might be Mr. Bingley since he is so amiable." His lips curled into a small teasing smile and his eyes twinkled. "I mean him no ill, but he is not the most studious of men." The smile grew. "And I may not even gain him as a son unless he, or one of his friends, can convince Jane he is not fickle."

Darcy shook his head, a small smile curling his lips. "Indeed, I hope that if your daughter's happiness depends upon it, it can be accomplished. However, it must be noted that this particular friend, though he may do all he can to convince Miss Bennet of Mr. Bingley's worth and innocence, is not known for his eloquence with the Bennet ladies."

Mr. Bennet reached across the carriage as it drew to a stop and patted Darcy's knee much like a solicitous father might. "Ah," he said with a wink, "but you are learning."

Chapter 9

London

Lydia folded her arms and stood in front of Wickham, blocking his path to the establishment behind her. People bustled in and out of the inn. One young gentleman paused for a moment, looking curiously at the pair before moving on. A maid slowed her steps as she passed them, and Wickham's lips curled into a smile as he winked at the young girl. Lydia rolled her eyes and shook her head. Staying here as Wickham had suggested would not do.

"You will take me and my maid," Lydia waved a hand at the poor frightened servant, who stood fidgeting behind her mistress, "to Derbyshire. My sisters are there, and I wish to join their fun."

"I will do no such thing," he said, taking a step to the side.

She placed herself between him and the inn once again. "I cannot stay here."

He shrugged. "Where you stay or where you go is none of my concern." There was no way he would willingly go to Derbyshire. Mr. Williams had told him that to show his face again in the area would likely lead to unpleasantness, and old Williams was just the man to ensure it happened. He might be the constable, but, rumor had it, he was not above seeing justice fulfilled outside of due process. His men had appeared rather suddenly after Tolson's accident last spring. He shook himself. No, Williams was not a man with whom he wished to trifle. Wickham appreciated life and wished to keep his.

And then there were Darcy and his cousin, Fitzwilliam. After last summer's botched play for Miss Darcy's inheritance — well, it was best if he stayed clear of those gentlemen. Darcy would likely not kill him, but he could not guarantee the good colonel would not find a way to follow through on the threats he had snarled at Ramsgate. Wickham had been enduring the constant glares and sudden appearances of that man at Brighton. More than one amorous rendezvous had been scuttled due to him. Wickham was looking forward to a few days without supervision.

Lydia matched Wickham's step to the side again. He could not leave her here on the streets of London when she needed to find her way to Derbyshire! He simply could not. She had expected a bit more cooperation from him than a flat refusal. He had always willingly done what she asked before. It was not an eventuality for which she had not prepared, but it was not exactly what she had expected.

"I cannot go to Derbyshire," said Wickham. "Town is my destination, and I'll go no farther."

Lydia fluttered her eyelashes and smiled. It was a technique that had worked before. Perhaps it might be more effective now than just demanding. "Oh, but you must."

He shook his head. He was not going one mile closer to Derbyshire unless forced, and he doubted very much that the feather-brained chit before him would be able to force him to do anything. He smiled as her smile turned to a frown before becoming something of an indifferent pout.

Well, if it must come to that, it must be done. Lydia flicked a piece of lint from her sleeve. "I am afraid you are wrong, and you must see me to Derbyshire."

"I do not see why I must," he replied, trying once again to slip around her and being thwarted by her matching his move. Agitation showed plainly on his face.

"Well, you see," Lydia began, smiling lightly while watching Wickham's face carefully. That look of displeasure was certain to deepen in a moment, and she must watch for signs of anything more than words being hurled at her. "I know that you cheated Saunders out of money last week." Her smile widened. "I have it in writing. Not your own, mind you, but a very close representation. The signature, however, is yours."

Wickham's brows drew together, and his mouth dropped open slightly. "You forged a note?"

She shrugged and fluttered her lashes again, feigning as innocent a look as she could. If her expression were to be honest, it would have been one of delight at having surprised someone who thought himself so clever. "Forged is such an ugly word. I prefer created. It really is not hard to do, you know. I can copy all my sisters' writing."

Wickham answered her charming smile with

one of his own as he glanced around their surroundings. "I could just take it from you," he said quietly while eyeing her reticule.

She held her bag out towards him. It was an action that once again startled him according to his expression. Although she had not expected to have to use her full plan, she was finding it quite delightful to do so. There was something exhilarating about matching wits with another. Perhaps this was why Elizabeth was always debating?

Lydia wished to spend a moment contemplating that startling idea, but there was not time. She needed to convince Wickham to take her to Derbyshire and the sooner the better. Since he had not taken her reticule, she pulled it back, opened it, and looked inside.

"Oh, I do not have it with me." She closed her bag. "But then having it with me would be foolish, would it not? It could get lost or stolen." She giggled. "Kitty has it."

Her smile faded as his scowl darkened. It was time to tell him the whole of just how much he should wish to assist her. "Along with the note about your cheating, she also has two letters of distress from me accusing you of threatening to harm me that she is to give to my father and Mr. Darcy."

"Darcy?" Wickham's brows rose in surprise.

"He did not seem to like you." She had not seen anyone look at another with such hatred as Mr. Darcy had looked at Wickham when they met him on the road from Meryton. And, knowing Mr. Darcy was a wealthy man and more than a little enamoured with Elizabeth, she doubted he would spare any expense in seeing to her rescue. She might not enjoy the man's grave countenance, but he was a true gentleman, no matter what Elizabeth might say to the contrary.

Wickham snorted. No, Darcy did not like him. He rather knew that the man hated him. "It does not take a great deal of observation to know that."

His reticence to fall into line with her wishes was beginning to annoy her, but she would not allow him to know, of course. So, she shrugged one shoulder with as much nonchalance as she could muster. "It does not matter if it took an extraordinary amount of deduction or just a trifle. I am certain he will act accordingly if he hears you have endangered me." She fluttered her eyelashes again.

Darcy's parting words when he left Ramsgate played in Wickham's mind. "I will save you this once, but should I hear of a word of this being spoken to anyone or if you should attempt to prey on another lady of my acquaintance, I will allow Fitzwilliam to do as he wishes." A letter suggesting any sort of injury to Lydia reaching Darcy would not be in Wickham's best interest.

"You do not have the directions to send such a letter, and he shall not be returning to Hertfordshire, I should say. He liked very few in the area, and there is nothing to draw him back since his friend seems unlikely to return."

He really did not think anyone could best him, did he? Lydia sighed. "Do not take me for a simpleton, Mr. Wickham. I am the youngest of five sisters, and I know how to get what I want. I assure you I have addressed the missive appropriately. Kitty will send it in five days' time if she has not heard from me, and I will not write to her until you and I have reached Derbyshire."

Wickham stared down at the silly chit with disgust. She had given no indication that such a devious plan, or any plan for that matter, could be formulated in her pretty little head. "Very well," he muttered through clenched teeth. "We will leave in the morning."

She shook her head. "No, we will leave now."

"We cannot go until there is a coach on which we can buy passage. I have no desire to go looking for one at this moment as I have friends I wish to see." He pushed her to the side.

Lydia followed behind. "But you will drink, and then you will sleep too long." He was always indulging more than he should. If he did not drink so much as he did, his list of debts would not be nearly so long as it was. He was admirably clever when sober, but his wits failed him quickly in the presence of alcohol.

Wickham ignored her and pushed open the door to the inn where he always took a room when in town.

She growled to herself. She did not like to be ignored, nor did she like not having her way. If he thought he could have his way by denying her hers, he was sadly mistaken. She slid up beside him, wound her arm around his, and laid her head on his shoulder as he spoke to the innkeeper.

"Do make it sure it has a comfortable bed, Wickham dear," she inserted into the conversation as sweetly as she could.

"Up the stairs and to the right. Same as always." The innkeeper took the money Wickham gave him and then handed Wickham the key.

"Molly Benson," she introduced herself to the portly man, who was looking at her curiously. "We are on our way to Scotland," she whispered loudly, placing a hand on her belly. "Papa would not agree to our marriage you see, but it really must happen soon, for it would be best if Papa thinks the little one was born a few weeks early." She rubbed her stomach in a circular motion as she had seen many expectant women do. "Mama had two which were early you know, so it would not be so far a stretch to think that I take after her and that this one was also early, now would it?" She blinked wide eyes at the man.

"I am so dreadfully happy to be out of that coach. The motion was nearly more than I could handle, but Wickham has promised to spend the evening reading to me, so I shall be fine by morning." She held her hand out to her maid, who handed her the book she had been holding since they disembarked from the coach. "My favourite." Lydia sighed. "And his voice is so melodic." She smiled up at Wickham. His face was suffused with shock, and it nearly caused her to giggle. "See that our dinner is sent to our room," she said to the innkeeper, who mumbled something in agreement.

Wickham opened his mouth to speak and fearing that he might attempt to refute what she had said, she added, "I fear I may be too exhausted to write that letter to my sister." She removed her arm from his and stretched and yawned.

Wickham's eyes narrowed, but he remained silent as they ascended the stairs to the room they had been assigned. He pushed open the door and waited for her to enter, but she remained in the hall. She would not be locked in a room while he enjoyed his evening and most likely made his escape. She smiled at him and motioned for him to enter, which, after considering her with a hard stare for a few minutes, he did. Then, she followed.

"I will have my way, Mr. Wickham," she said as she closed the door and slid the bolt across.

"And perhaps, I will have mine," he shot back.

She shook her head. "I am afraid not, Mr. Wickham. For if you were to ruin me in truth, you would then have to marry me in truth, and I will not marry you."

"Plenty of ladies are not maidens when they marry," he said, taking a step closer to her.

"This one intends to be." She folded her arms across her chest and refused to be moved. She would not be bullied into appearing weak. However, she did hope that should he be even more of a scoundrel than she thought, Margaret, her maid, would set off a cry of alarm. But, to her relief, he held his ground and did not advance any further.

"You? You, who flutters your lashes at any handsome man and displays your assets to best garner a gentleman's attention?" He laughed.

She placed her hands on her hips and glared at him. A flirt she might be, but that did not make her a light skirt. "Do you not practice marching and shooting?"

"Of course," he replied.

"For what purpose? To start a fight on a Saturday night for entertainment?"

He gave her a puzzled look. "No, so we might be prepared for a fight should one arise, and because if we do not, our colonel might have us flogged."

Lydia shrugged and went to sit in one of the chairs next to the small table in the room. "I practice so that when a worthy gentleman crosses my path, I shall be ready to conquer him." She laughed. "And I do not go beyond flirting because I do not wish for my father to flog me with his lectures." She motioned to the other chair. "You should make yourself comfortable. No one will be expecting you to leave your room this evening. You are reading to your future wife, after all." She sighed. "This is so much better than spending the evening and night in a carriage, is it not?"

It was not. Neither Wickham nor Lydia enjoyed the evening nor the night, and both rose early the next morning — Wickham from the bed, and Lydia from the mat she had fashioned on the floor before the door — and were well on their way to Derbyshire before her father and Mr. Darcy entered London.

Chapter 10

Mr. Bennet watched Mr. Darcy give directions to his staff as they entered the house. Two footmen were to attend him in his study as soon as could be managed, while a meal was to be laid out in the library. Maids were sent scurrying, preparing a room for their guest. Mr. Bennet's hat and coat were taken from him, and within ten minutes of arriving at the door to Darcy House, he found himself comfortably seated in a study double the size of his own. The walls were filled with just as many books as his were, but here, everything had a more orderly appearance. Piles of papers sat neatly on the desk, some in wooden boxes.

Darcy saw Mr. Bennet eying the boxes of papers and with a sheepish grin explained, "I need things in their place, or I find I get lost. Some have the ability to have things combined in one pile and can remember exactly where an item is, but I cannot. Lists, files, and schedules are of great importance to me. I find I am quite lost without a plan."

Mr. Bennet nodded. "My Lizzy is rather the opposite. You should be warned. Do not misunderstand me, she can keep a book as well as anyone and organize with the best, but it is not her natural tendency. You may find you will need patience with her."

Darcy smiled. "I have some experience with those not given to naturally ordering things. You must remember Bingley is my friend," he paused and then added with a sigh, "at least, he is currently my friend." He took a stack of correspondence from one box and sorted it. Most of the letters were returned to the box, while a few were placed in front of Darcy on the desk. "These, I must attend to myself," he explained, "although the matters, I am sure, are not pressing, so they will travel with me. The others are merely invitations that will need to be declined by my man."

"Sir," one footman, followed by a second, entered the study. "Mr. Thompson said you wished to see us."

Darcy nodded and motioned for them to take a

seat. Thompson had chosen well. These two were probably the largest footmen on his staff. Both were tall and muscular, and neither appeared to be too well-bred to be entering the areas Darcy was about to ask them to enter.

"I need to find someone," he began when the two men were seated somewhat uncomfortably before his desk.

Very few of his servants were ever summoned to his office. Most requests were passed on to them through his butler or housekeeper. However, this was not a topic which could be carried from one person to another. It needed to be contained as much as possible if he wished to keep Lydia's reputation from being further damaged.

"Mr. Bennet's daughter has made an unexpected trip to town," Darcy continued.

"With a scoundrel," muttered Mr. Bennet.

Darcy nodded his agreement with the evaluation of Wickham and then explained the nature of task he wished his men to accomplish, scratched out some addresses on a paper, and after a short rummage through a drawer on the bookcase behind his desk, showed them a miniature of Wickham. "It is rather urgent that we find him as soon as possible, as Miss Bennet's father is desirous to have her back unharmed."

"Of course, sir," both men replied as they stood to leave.

"It is to be private?" asked the second footman.

"As private as a matter such as this can be," acknowledged Darcy. "If you find them, you are to return here and tell us. You do not need to apprehend them, unless, of course, you come upon them as they are leaving. There will, of course, be a bit extra in your pay for doing this for me whether you find them or not."

"Thank you, sir," said the first footman and then turning to Mr. Bennet, he added. "We will do our best."

"As if she were me own sister," muttered the second before he turned and followed the other footman from the room.

Darcy rose from his chair. "And now we wait." He gathered the letters from his desk and walked toward the study door. "I thought the library might be the best place to while away our time. We might not hear back for hours."

"Do you still expect Mr. Bingley?" asked Mr. Bennet as they stepped into the corridor.

Darcy nodded his reply before turning to his butler. "Thompson, well done on the footmen." He handed him the few letters he carried. "Please see that these are placed with my things in my room. I should be packed and ready for a journey in the morning."

"Of course, sir," replied Thompson.

"And, when Mr. Bingley arrives, please show him to the library."

"As you wish, sir. Your meal is waiting, sir."

A small table of cold meat, cheese, rolls and ale had been set out next to a grouping of chairs in the middle of the large room. A further tray of sweets and port sat on a second table, also within the grouping. It was the meal Darcy often took, in smaller quantity, when he arrived home from traveling. He picked up a piece of cheese from the plate and popped it into his mouth as he took a seat and waited for Mr. Bennet to join him. It had been a long day, and despite his concern regarding Lydia, Darcy was hungry. He chuckled to himself as the gentleman turned about, looking at the shelves of books very much like a child might survey a tray of cakes.

"Indeed, my favourite son," Mr. Bennet

mumbled as he finally pulled himself from his admiration of the room. "I must say, I am glad you were able to convince my daughter to accept you," he said to Darcy with a grin.

Darcy returned the smile. "As am I, sir. As am I."

They were just tucking into a second helping of food and ale when Bingley was announced.

"Ah, Darcy!" said Bingley as he entered the room. "Mr. Bennet!" His surprise was evident both in his tone and the falter in his steps. "It...it is good to see you, sir," he said in greeting.

"No need to try to hide your surprise, my boy. I am as surprised to be here as you are to see me, but," he leaned back in his chair and gave Darcy an amused smile, "I shall leave the explanation of that to your friend."

Darcy shifted uneasily in his chair. "You are alone?"

"Caroline wished to accompany me, but I managed to escape without her."

"Good," muttered Mr. Bennet. Then, with a sheepish smile, he added, "I do apologize, but I am rather liking being free of females for a time."

Bingley waved it away with a laugh. "We are all happy to be free of Caroline. Am I right, Darcy?"

Darcy shrugged and reluctantly nodded. "Especially tonight." He finished his ale. "I have something to tell you that is not easily done." He rose and paced to the window and back. "It will no doubt be shocking, and I ask that you allow me to finish before you respond."

Bingley's brows furrowed. "I cannot imagine what you might have done that would be shocking, but I agree."

"I truly wish you did not hold me in such high esteem, Bingley." Pain coloured Darcy's words. "It makes it more difficult to admit my errors and how I might have harmed you."

Bingley's brows rose, and he pointed to himself as if questioning whether or not he had heard the statement correctly.

"Yes, you," said Darcy with a sad smile. He paced to the window and back. "I am not sure how to begin," he admitted.

Mr. Bennet leaned forward in his chair. "He is marrying Elizabeth. Lydia has run off, so we must find her, and Jane, whom you were convinced did not love you, did. I cannot say she still does, but she did." He leaned back in his chair once again.

Darcy stared at him, mouth agape.

Mr. Bennet shrugged. "You needed help. I admit it is not the most gentle way to present the news, but we are all men here. And friends." He looked pointedly at Mr. Bingley and emphasized the word. "There is no need to take the long way around as I would with my wife or daughters. I think we are made of sterner stuff than that."

He rose and motioned for Darcy to sit. "I know I said I would leave this to your friend to explain, but I cannot do it." He chuckled. "I suppose it is not only my wife who likes to meddle, though I do hope my meddling is more productive and useful than hers." He held up a finger as Bingley opened his mouth to speak.

"Love is a sneaky creature. You, Mr. Bingley, are not so easily caught unawares by it. In fact, I would venture a guess that you often think you see it when it is not there." He raised an eyebrow at Bingley and waited for him to agree that such was the case. "However, Mr. Darcy, here, I would dare to say, rarely sees her approach and quite likely never expected her to threaten him at all. Or, mayhap, he did and that is why he wears his scowl so often — as an attempt to scare her away."

Bingley chuckled.

Mr. Bennet with a small chuckle of his own continued without giving Darcy a moment to accept or deny the charges. "He has been well-chastised for his error on your behalf, Mr. Bingley. My Lizzy is not one to allow her sister to be treated ill without showing her displeasure to the one she holds accountable." He chuckled again. "I am not sure how she discovered Mr. Darcy's role in the whole charade, but she did and listed it among other reasons for refusing him."

"But?" Bingley's brows were furrowed deeply in confusion.

Mr. Bennet winked and smiled at him. "The first time he offered. In the spring, was it?" He waited for Darcy to confirm this. Then, he took a seat, leaned toward Bingley, and, growing serious, added, "For several months, your friend has tried to reorder his thinking and his life in such a way as to overcome the pain of such a refusal. It is the same pain from which he was attempting to keep you safe — mistaken as he was. He had your best interests in mind." He leaned back. "My advice, young man, is to accept his apology when he offers it, and then decide if your heart still prefers Jane or if it was merely a pretty face and pleasant smile that

held your attention for a time but not for all time."
He sighed. "I will not see her heart broken again,"
he warned.

Darcy's chest clenched at the words. He shook
his head. "I doubt I have ever been so wrong about
anything in my entire life."

"Wickham," muttered Mr. Bennet.

Darcy's shoulders sagged. "True. I should revise
my words to say that when I am wrong, I am quite
dreadfully wrong. Perhaps it is a mistake to trust
me with your daughter."

Mr. Bennet shook his head. "She'll not let you go
so wrong, so long as you listen to her." He smiled
sheepishly at Darcy.

Darcy nodded his understanding while Bingley
looked at the two men in confusion.

"That bit has to do with Lydia," Mr. Bennet
explained.

"I cannot tell you, Bingley, how greatly my heart
has grieved over my actions toward both you and
Miss Bennet. I did not know what pain I caused
until Miss Elizabeth turned me away." He shook
his head. "I am not sure I could forgive someone
who had treated me so, but I would be very grateful
if you would forgive me this wrong." His breath

caught in his chest as he waited for Bingley to respond.

Bingley looked at Darcy and then Mr. Bennet, who gave him a nod and tilted his head toward Darcy as if telling him to accept the apology.

"She loved me?" Bingley asked.

"That is what Miss Elizabeth says," Darcy replied.

"But she may not now?"

Darcy's heart sighed at Bingley's sad tone.

"If it was love," said Mr. Bennet softly, "then she still will. If it was not, then you are far better off to have a season of pain rather than a lifetime of it."

Bingley sadly nodded his acceptance of the fact and turned to Darcy. "You thought you were helping me?"

"I did."

"Never, for the rest of our lives, ever help me in such a fashion again. If I require your help with relationships, I will ask for it — though not for some time, I should think."

"I am forgiven?" Relief, nearly certain that forgiveness had been granted, crept cautiously into Darcy's heart.

"I should hate to ask a father for his daughter's

hand," Bingley explained, "if I am so fortunate as to gain her permission to do so, when he knows that I was unwilling to take his advice. So, yes, you are forgiven."

Darcy blew out a great breath as relief swelled within him.

Mr. Bennet smiled at them both. "So much easier than daughters." He looked to the tray of sweets. "Some port before we explain about Lydia?"

Darcy agreed and was just handing a glass to Bingley before taking his own when...

"Darcy!" A bellow carried from the entry.

Must Richard always make such a loud entrance? "My cousin," he explained to Mr. Bennet.

"Nearly as loud as my wife," muttered Mr. Bennet with a smile and a wink. "Probably not as fetching in a dress, however."

Darcy and Bingley chuckled.

"Darcy!" There was an impatience to the repeated bellow followed by a tromping of feet growing louder as they approached the library.

A frazzled Thompson scurried into the room

behind Colonel Fitzwilliam. "I tried to explain, sir."

"It is quite alright. Richard is more familiar with giving than receiving orders." Darcy glowered at his cousin, who, at least, had the decency to look somewhat embarrassed. "Mr. Bennet, my cousin, Colonel Fitzwilliam. Richard, Mr. Bennet. Do come in and sit down." He motioned to a chair and added, "And kindly keep your voice to a low rumble."

"I haven't time," Richard replied. "I am looking for a good-for-nothing wastrel for Forrester, and my leave does not start until I find both him and the young lady he took with him." Richard paced a small path in front of the door. His hands clenched and unclenched behind his back. "I need the address of that inn where you said he was last time we needed to find him."

"Sit," Darcy barked the order and Richard complied. "We are just awaiting the men I sent to that very inn. Mr. Bennet is as anxious to have his daughter returned as you are to begin your leave. Will you be spending it in town?"

Once again, Richard looked rather chagrinned.

"I apologize. I did not put the name of the young lady and yours together."

Mr. Bennet uncrossed his legs and crossed them again, this time with the left foot on top of the right. "I apologize for my daughter being a cause for your current assignment. She is a headstrong child — smart, but willful. Again, I must apologize for that."

"Ah, I nearly forgot." Richard reached into his pocket. "This is for you," he said handing a letter to Darcy. "There was a man on the steps when I arrived," he explained as Darcy looked at the address with some confusion.

Darcy turned the letter over in his hands and ran a finger over the seal, unsure if he should read this now or wait until later.

"Read it," said Richard. "You'll be half distracted until you do. Am I not right, Bingley?"

"Oh, indeed," agreed Bingley.

Mr. Bennet raised a brow. "From a gentleman or lady?" he inquired, a slight smirk pulling at his mouth.

"Mr. Dobney," Darcy replied. "Philip," he added to Bingley before explaining to Mr. Bennet who Philip was.

Mr. Bennet chuckled as Darcy turned the letter over in his hands while speaking. "You will not offend me if you tend to your letter. I am the one inconveniencing you with my presence, after all. If it were not for Lydia, I would not be here at all."

Darcy insisted that Mr. Bennet was not an inconvenience, although Mr. Bennet would hear nothing of being untruthful out of politeness. This, of course, led to a discussion of a polite dissimulation and the ills or benefits of such pretense. As Richard waxed eloquent on a third story of the ills of such actions, Darcy excused himself to read his letter. He knew that Richard, once started on a topic, could continue for some time, and that the stories were, without a doubt, ones which Darcy had heard before.

Darcy,

As I have promised, I am writing to inform you of a new arrival in the area. My cousin, Captain Harris, has arrived for a visit. He has called on Willow Hall with my sister. In fact, that is where Lucy and I found him this afternoon — lounging in the garden with the full family. Miss Bennet and the Gardiners have arrived safely. You will be pleased to know that Harris has shown no particular attention to Miss Elizabeth. He does, however, seem taken with Miss Bennet, and I cannot blame him. She is quite lovely.

I am to inform you, for Lucy says I must, that your Miss Elizabeth has eyes only for you, so you need not worry. Lucy also wishes you to know that Miss Elizabeth has had the full story of all that transpired with Lucy's uncle and Wickham. It seems Miss Elizabeth's youngest sister has gone to Brighton and has, according to Harris, been flirting with several officers — Wickham being one of them. You might wish to share what you know of the man with Mr. Bennet when you call on him. If this letter reaches you after you have called on him, I would urge you to write to him. Lucy gives permission to speak of her ordeal.

Looking forward to your return, etc.

P.D.

"Is all well in Derbyshire?" asked Richard as Darcy folded the letter.

Darcy grimaced slightly. "Just informing me that Miss Bennet and the Gardiners have arrived safely, as has Captain Harris. It seems Harris has brought news from Brighton that Miss Elizabeth found unsettling."

"About Lydia?" asked Mr. Bennet.

Darcy nodded slowly. "It seems Harris mentioned some flirtation." Darcy motioned for the footmen, who stood at the door, to enter. "What have you discovered?"

The two men looked at each other uneasily.

"They all know of it," assured Darcy. "You may speak freely."

"They were not at the inn when we arrived, but they had been there, sir," began the first man. "They left this morning."

"They are going to Scotland, sir," said the second man. "It seems they must marry."

Darcy's heart sank to his boots. "They must?" he asked.

The second man cleared his throat. "Yes, sir. It seems the lady is with child."

Chapter 11

Derbyshire

"We have another guest, ma'am," said Mrs. Smith, entering the drawing room where the ladies of Willow Hall had gathered to sew and chat with Lucy, Mary Ellen, and Georgiana.

"Another?" asked Cecily.

"Miss Lydia Bennet, ma'am."

Elizabeth's mouth dropped open as she gasped. "Lydia is here?"

"Yes, miss," replied Mrs. Smith. Elizabeth could tell by the look on the housekeeper's face that she was not entirely pleased with the new arrival. "She's waiting in the entry. Shall I show her in?"

"Oh, indeed." Cecily tucked her sewing back into her workbasket. "We can't have her standing in the entryway, nor can we turn her out."

"Is she unaccompanied?" asked Aunt Gardiner.

Mrs. Smith shook her head. "There is an officer with her." Her eyes narrowed and her lips puckered slightly in disgust. "Lieutenant Wickham."

Elizabeth was certain her heart had stopped beating for a moment. It could not be. It just could not be. She cast an uneasy glance at Lucy and Georgiana before rising and hurrying from the room. She needed to see the truth of the report for herself.

"Lydia!" she said in surprise. Her sister and Wickham were indeed in the entryway. "What are you doing here? Why are you not in Brighton?"

Lydia pouted. This was not exactly the welcome she had expected. They would be surprised, to be sure, but not displeased. "Are you not glad to see me? I thought you and Jane and Aunt would be delighted. I have gone to an enormous amount of trouble to come for a visit." She crossed her arms. Lizzy was nearly as severe as Mary at times; perhaps the others would be more welcoming.

"How can I be happy you are here when you are supposed to be in Brighton?"

"Brighton is dull." Lydia tried not to reply to her sister's critical tone without snapping, but it was not possible.

"Dull?" Elizabeth repeated incredulously.

"Yes, Brighton is dull, which is why I asked Mr. Wickham if he would escort me to visit you." She flashed a sweet smile at Elizabeth and managed, this time, to keep her tone pleasant. "It was ever so long a journey. I had not realized just how far Derbyshire is from Hertfordshire. It is quite a distance, is it not?"

"Indeed, it is." Elizabeth wished to grab her sister by the shoulders and shake the smile from her face. Had she no idea the impropriety of her actions? "You travelled alone?" She raised a brow and looked at Wickham for an answer.

"No," he replied. "Miss Lydia was accompanied by a maid, and we were on a crowded coach."

"Oh, Lizzy! It was very unpleasant. All those people bouncing around and bumping into one another." Lydia shuddered dramatically. "I shall not like to do that again. It is much better to have one's own carriage."

By this time, Mrs. Abbot had joined Elizabeth in the hall.

"Come," said Cecily. "This would be a far more pleasant conversation to have in the sitting room." She turned to Mrs. Smith. "Please have Mr. Abbot and Mr. Gardiner join us at their earliest convenience."

"I cannot stay," said Wickham.

"You'll stay." There was a steeliness to Cecily's voice. "Until we have this all sorted out, you will stay, sir."

"But I am not welcome –" Wickham attempted again to extricate himself from his present situation, but Cecily would not allow it.

"You most certainly are not, but that does not signify." She turned to Elizabeth. "Take Lydia to the sitting room. Mr. Wickham and I shall follow as soon as I have a word with him."

Elizabeth did as instructed and had gotten both Lydia and herself into seats before Cecily, accompanied by a somber Wickham, entered. Wickham bowed and greeted each person in turn and then took a seat away from the group of ladies.

Jane was asking Lydia about Mrs. Forrester and the sites of Brighton, and Elizabeth was thankful for it. For the conversation filled what otherwise would have surely been a silent room. Georgiana's eyes did not leave her stitching, and Lucy's did not leave Georgiana. Elizabeth found herself watching

Lydia for a moment and then Wickham, who was nervously turning his hat in his hands.

"I would have been here sooner, but Mr. Wickham insisted on calling on some stuffy old friend first."

Elizabeth turned her eyes back to Lydia. "And who was that?" she inquired.

"Mr. Williams," Wickham answered. "I needed to see him. I had promised him that I would call on him first if I ever came back to Derbyshire. It was a promise I dared not break."

"He was such a crosspatch," said Lydia. "I did not think he would let us continue on our way."

"He is the constable," said Lucy. "He is only cross when he needs to be. Normally, he is a rather pleasant fellow."

"The constable?" asked Lydia in surprise.

Wickham glowered at her. "I told you when we were in London that I was not welcome here. I did not lie."

Lydia crossed her arms and scowled at him in return. "Well, it is quite difficult to ferret out when you are lying and when you are not. Perhaps if you were honest more often."

"Ah, Lydia," said Mr. Gardiner, entering the

room ahead of Mr. Abbot. "I heard you had arrived. You are well?" He tilted his head to the side and looked at her.

"I am," she replied.

"Tell me of your journey," Mr. Gardiner said as he took a seat near his wife. "Did you meet any interesting people along the way?"

His tone was open and engaging, but Elizabeth noted how he seemed to force his smile and knew that his manners were to elicit the full story from Lydia. She listened for a few moments as Lydia spoke of her departure from Brighton and her stop in London.

"An inn?" The words leapt from Elizabeth's mouth. "You spent a night in an inn with him?" She waved her hand in Wickham's direction. "Have you no idea of propriety?"

"He refused to continue on. I had no option other than sleeping in the street, and I did not give the innkeeper my name." Lydia crossed her arms and scowled at Elizabeth.

Elizabeth huffed and shook her head.

"Perhaps a walk in the garden?" suggested Cecily. "We must hear the full tale, you know," she added softly.

Elizabeth nodded her understanding.

"I would walk with you," Georgiana offered.

"As would I," said Lucy, rising. "In fact, I would like a bit of air. Mary Ellen, will you join us?"

Elizabeth rose to follow the three from the room. Mary Ellen joined arms with Georgiana, and Lucy took Elizabeth's but remained standing near the house until the others were a distance ahead.

"Now," she said with a smile, "tell me what is in your heart."

"She will have to marry him." Elizabeth blinked against the tears that formed in her eyes.

"She may," agreed Lucy. "It would be an unfortunate result but not unlikely. Do you worry for her safety or her happiness?"

Elizabeth nodded. "How could one be happy with such a man? How could one be safe?" A tear slid down her cheek. "If I had not listened to him, if I had not befriended him, this would not have happened."

Lucy drew her close. "He is handsome, and you said she was a flirt. Is it truly impossible that it could not have happened on its own?" Lucy led her to a bench near a tree as Elizabeth allowed that it was not entirely outside the realm of possibility.

They sat silently for a few moments. Lucy watched as grief played at Elizabeth's features. There was yet something ˌwhich was disquieting her, and Lucy feared that she knew all too well what it was, for she had, thanks to her uncle, felt the same — twice. So, it was not so very surprising when Elizabeth finally shook her head and voiced her true concern.

"I cannot bear to think of Georgiana having to be related to him, and I cannot imagine her brother would wish it." She drew a shuddering breath as tears flowed down her cheeks. "Lydia has not only destroyed her own happiness but mine as well."

Somewhere between London and Derbyshire

Darcy settled into the carriage again once the fresh horses had been acquired.

"I am not so old that I could not ride a horse," grumbled Mr. Bennet.

Darcy was unsure how many times he had heard the complaint.

"Richard and Bingley are riding ahead of us, and we shall travel as quickly as we can, but the carriage was needed." Darcy had said the same words each time Mr. Bennet had grumbled and shifted uneasily, but this time, he added, "we can ride from Pemberley."

Mr. Bennet nodded and attempted to open his book to occupy his mind. Darcy watched as the man flipped pages and then went back and flipped them again before closing the book and placing it on the bench next to him.

"What a fool I have been," Mr. Bennet leaned his head against the back of the carriage. "How could I have allowed her to go to Brighton? Was my peace truly worth the cost?" His eyes continued to search the top of the carriage as if it would give him the answers he sought.

"A lady of fifteen or sixteen can be persuasive," Darcy replied. "I had wished for my sister to wait for me to accompany her to Ramsgate, but the thought so distressed her that I pushed my better judgement to the side and allowed her to go ahead of me. It was not as if she would be unaccompanied. She had a companion who seemed respectable." He shrugged as Mr. Bennet looked his direction. "I did not know Mrs. Younge's connection to Wickham, and you did not know Wickham's true character. We, both of us, made decisions based on what we knew. Unfortunately, those decisions proved poor."

He shook his head at his foolishness in condemning Mr. Bennet for his neglect of family. True, the man did not appear to put forth enough effort — and Darcy was sure there were improvements that begged making. However, Darcy could commiserate to a degree with the gentleman. "I struggle to do right by one sister. I cannot imagine how much more challenging it would be to have five."

"You are far too generous," Mr. Bennet replied with a sad smile. "It is a challenge, and there are six females in my home, not five." He chuckled. "You are gaining a sensible wife, so your task of raising children, should they all be girls, will be much easier." He turned to look out at the road. The sun was dipping behind the hills and the shadows were growing. "I trusted my wife to guide them. What did I know of daughters? I had only a brother and a cousin." He smiled at Darcy. "My mother was much like Lizzy — a quick wit, a strong character, a love of learning, and a temper strong enough to quell the most stubborn acquaintance who dared challenge her." He chuckled again at the memory.

"You were close to her?"

"Closer to her than to my father." He sighed. "There was no love lost between my father and me. He preferred my brother and my cousin. They questioned less."

The sound of the wheels on the road and the rhythmic fall of horses' hooves filled the carriage for some minutes.

"That is why the estate is entailed," Mr. Bennet said, at last. "My father figured I would do a miserable job of seeing to it. He despised my love of new methods, you see." His chuckle, this time, was a bitter one. "And to my brother and my cousin, it looked like I was fulfilling my father's predictions." An impertinent grin very like Lizzy's played at his mouth. "The estate does well."

Darcy's brows rose. "Why hide your success?"

Mr. Bennet shrugged. "I cared not for their opinion and felt they deserved to keep it. I also did not trust my cousin and feared that if he knew I was a success, he might hasten my demise. He was with my brother when my brother had his fall. That is when the rift in our family occurred. I held him responsible since it was his idea to go out in foul weather. Fortunately, he has not survived me and will not reap the benefits of my labours. Unfortunately, his brother's son will. I would rather the estate not go to such a bumbling fool, but he seems harmless enough if you can avoid his prattling." He smiled. "And Charlotte is a fine young woman. She will do well by the estate and him. Not that I envy her the task."

The sounds of travel once again filled the space between the two men. Darcy considered the man across from him. There was much he had assumed about him, but the more time he spent with Mr. Bennet, the more he realized that not all of his assumptions were true. Again, he shook his head. How much more clearly he saw things since Elizabeth's refusal had caused him to re-evaluate himself and all he knew.

"She did well with the first two, and to a point with Mary." Mr. Bennet's head was resting against the back of the carriage. "But she became overwhelmed when the fourth was another girl." He looked toward Darcy for a moment. "She thought herself a failure, and no matter my assurance, she would not change from her position."

He leaned his head back again. "She was as beautiful as Jane and as lively as Lydia. She still is beautiful, but her liveliness has been misdirected, and I have been unsuccessful in redirecting it."

He drew a deep breath and released it. "That was my error, Mr. Darcy. I allowed myself to accept the failure. My distress is not so much about a poor decision in allowing Lydia to journey to Brighton, although it was unwise." He shook his head. "No, my distress is from allowing myself to find comfort in solitude while my wife seeks comfort in promoting her daughters — in an unchecked fashion. And now, I must feel the full weight of that decision, knowing that it will bring sorrow to my wife and daughters."

"Perhaps, we will overtake them." Darcy knew it was unlikely and even if they did, the damage had already been done.

Mr. Bennet shook his head. "She is with child, and even is she was not, her reputation is tarnished. She will have to marry the man." Mr. Bennet leaned forward. "I would understand if you were to withdraw your offer. I cannot expect you to wish the connection."

"Withdraw my offer?" The idea shocked Darcy. Not once in all of the events of the last two days had he considered such a thing. "I would rather be connected to ten men such as Wickham than to live without your daughter, sir."

Mr. Bennet patted Darcy's knee and then leaned his head against the back of the coach again as he prepared to get some rest. "If I have thought it, Lizzy will as well when she hears of what Lydia has done."

"Then we shall have to take the carriage and your daughter to Scotland with us, and we will marry before a word of this situation is spoken to her."

Mr. Bennet chuckled. "I applaud your determination, but I dare say you'll not get her to Gretna Green without her discovering the truth."

Chapter 12

Derbyshire

"Darcy will not give you up," said Lucy, placing an arm around Elizabeth's shoulders, "and if you are even considering rejecting him, . . . again . . . I shall be quite cross with you."

"But to be tied to Wickham!" cried Elizabeth. How could she ask him to be connected to such a person? It was not that she wished to give Darcy up, but she could not hold him to an agreement that would make him miserable.

"Wickham would be less of a burden for him to bear than losing you would be." Lucy sighed and searched her mind for ways to convince Elizabeth of this truth. Finally, after listening for a few moments to Elizabeth's soft sobs, she decided to share what she knew of Darcy's letters.

"He was beyond despondent after you rejected

him." Her words were soft but drew Elizabeth's attention. "Philip feared for him."

"Feared?" Elizabeth sniffled and dried her eyes.

"Philip said Darcy sounded as if he was capable of doing himself harm, though he would not, for even in his distress he talked about those who were dependent on him." Lucy saw the pain her words were causing Elizabeth and squeezed her close.

"I would not tell you this if I did not think it beneficial." She gave Elizabeth a small smile. "He had not been so distraught over Georgiana's ordeal with Wickham. He was unpleasant to be around, to be sure. He was angry and ashamed, as well as worried for his sister, but never beyond what a good hard ride or an afternoon of chopping wood could not work away." She paused and then shook her head. "That is not entirely true. There was an air about him that was rather off-putting — a facade designed to keep everyone at a distance. His words could be quite cutting at times, but you know that." She was relieved to see Elizabeth's lips curve upwards just a bit at the comment.

"And then, he left for Hertfordshire to assist Bingley as planned, and his letters, which were at first very short, became longer, and his words became gentler. I remember in one that Philip read to me, he told of a lady who had a keen wit and was at the time of his writing, and much to his delight, engaging in a bit of debate about what one might consider an accomplished lady."

Elizabeth's mouth fell open slightly, and her eyes grew wide. She remembered well that afternoon at Netherfield.

"He was quite taken with you," Lucy continued, "so taken that he left Netherfield." She withdrew her arm from around Elizabeth's shoulders since it seemed as if Elizabeth had calmed for the moment.

"Even when he was in London, his letters still spoke of you. He could physically distance himself from you, but he could not separate you from his heart. That is how it is with love. Once it has laid claim to your heart, it cannot be easily removed, not even with well-thought out arguments concerning families or duties.

"Oh, the times I listened to Philip sigh and moan over the letters he wrote in return! He experienced such difficulty in counselling his friend that what one expects in a wife and what one finds are often quite different and that no matter what Darcy's family might expect of station or breeding in his wife, what Darcy desired and needed was far greater."

She took Elizabeth's hand, for the next part was necessarily going to be unsettling for her. "Finally, in one joyous letter, he announced that he had resolved to act as his heart desired. The young lady had once again been placed in his path, and he was determined to offer for her. We anxiously awaited his announcement to call the banns, but the next letter was nearly a month in coming — although we did have one before that from Georgiana telling us of her brother's state."

"Please, I cannot bear to hear it," Elizabeth said through fresh tears.

"But you must," Lucy spoke as gently as she could, though her tone was firm. She would not allow Elizabeth to cause the same pain to Darcy again. He was a friend, but beyond that she owed him so much for the help he provided her in dealing with her uncle. "His despair when we finally saw him was shocking. No amount of riding or chopping wood could dislodge it. It faded, but it was never gone. Even now, before he left for town, he was despondent at the thought of leaving —

fearful that he would lose you. He loves you completely. You mean more to him than an unfavourable connection. You must believe me."

Elizabeth stood and walked toward the tree that the Abbot boys loved to play under. Bits and pieces of Lucy's words replayed themselves in her mind. She leant against the tree and allowed her tears to fall without restraint. She knew she had injured Darcy with the words of her refusal — she had intended them to sting — but she had never imagined him to be so shaken by them. And now, she must either cause him the same unbearable pain or a slightly lesser one of being related to Wickham. How could she decide such a thing? If they did marry, would he grow to resent her because of her sister? As much as she could not bear the thought of not being his, the idea of being his and despised was equally as painful.

The sound of voices drew her from her contemplation, and she turned to look at the house, just as Jane, accompanied by Captain Harris and Mr. Dobney, entered the garden. She took a deep breath and, drying her eyes as best she could, returned to Lucy.

"We thought it best to join you," said Jane,

leaving the gentlemen near Lucy and walking a small distance away with her sister.

"How do things stand with Lydia?" asked Elizabeth.

"She is determined that she shall not marry Mr. Wickham." Jane sighed. "She says she has gone to great lengths to protect herself from such a thing happening, but it is Lydia, and though her plan is no doubt a clever one, it is not without fault. Uncle is still attempting to work on her."

"And what of Wickham?" Elizabeth asked.

"He had no part in the scheme beyond that which he was forced to take, and he does not seem willing to be wed to Lydia any more than she wishes to be tied to him. I do not know what can be done unless the matter can be silenced. Uncle will write to Papa tonight, and then, I suppose, we shall wait for his reply."

"And if Wickham leaves before Papa's answer arrives?"

Jane sighed. "That is a sticking point at present; however, Mr. Philip Dobney has gone to call for Mr. Williams, the constable, as he might have some sway."

"It is a fine mess," muttered Elizabeth.

"It is," admitted Jane. She glanced over her shoulder to where Lucy talked with her cousin and brother. "Are you well?"

Elizabeth shook her head. "I do not know until I know how Mr. Darcy will respond. Do Captain Harris and Mr. Dobney know what has happened?"

Jane sighed again. "Not the full tale, but enough. I believe any hope I had of capturing the captain may be at an end." She linked arms with Elizabeth and walked a bit further.

"And Mr. Dobney?" Elizabeth asked hopefully.

"He has yet to pay me any particular attention beyond the expected civilities," Jane said with a laugh. "I do not think our wayward sister shall inspire him to fall at my feet. Besides," she added softly, "what hope have I when you, though you have ensnared a man's heart as completely as you have Mr. Darcy's, fear losing his regard?"

"But there are different circumstances, a different relationship between Mr. Darcy and Mr. Wickham. You know there are."

"Perhaps," said Jane, "but Mr. Dobney and Captain Harris also have a relation who was ill-treated by the man."

"We are beyond hope, then?" asked Elizabeth.

"Never beyond hope," said Jane. "There must always be hope that happiness is not beyond our reach." She looked up toward the clouds that shifted back and forth in the sky above. "Even when the hope is very small."

~*~*~

Elizabeth rose from her bed as the sun stretched its arms across the fields, stirring the birds to sing and the night to flee. It had been a long night of little sleep. Her mind would not be quiet. It continually weighed Lucy's words about Darcy with the fears she had about bringing shame to him through her sister's actions.

She had wished to toss and turn in bed and considered rising and pacing the room, but Jane had fallen asleep with some difficulty, and Elizabeth had been loath to disturb her. So, she had waited, dozing briefly, disturbed in sleep by dreams and in waking moments by thought, until finally concluding in the end that it might be best to break with propriety and write a letter to Darcy, leaving the decision entirely with him.

So, quietly, she slipped from the room, wrapping her robe tightly about herself, and headed to the sitting room where she knew she would find writing supplies and a window that faced the early morning sun.

"Good morning," Mr. Abbot, who was bouncing Aiden on his knee, greeted her. "It is a rather early start to the day after the night we endured."

He smiled at Aiden and poked out his tongue. "I would still be in bed if it were not for this early riser. He was insistent that he see his mama but graciously agreed to spend time with his papa instead. I did not wish to disturb Cecily so early." He placed Aiden on the floor.

Aiden immediately pulled himself up next to his father's leg and stood, swaying slightly from side to side, lifting one foot and then the other before plopping down and beginning the process again.

"He is determined to be on his way," chuckled Mr. Abbot.

"He is," agreed Elizabeth. "I had hoped to write a letter before the day began." Elizabeth looked toward the writing desk.

Mr. Abbot made a small waving motion. "Do not let us keep you from your pleasure."

Elizabeth thanked him and seated herself at the desk.

"Gardiner wrote a letter to your father last night,

and I added my observations. It is not sealed yet. We wished to wait until morning — in case some thought for a solution would come after a few hours of rest. You may include yours with ours before we seal it."

Elizabeth held her pen still, hovering above the name she had just written. "I am not writing to Papa," she admitted softly.

"You are not?"

Elizabeth understood the surprise in Mr. Abbot's tone. To whom else would she be writing? Her mother was not to know of Lydia's tale until Mr. Bennet had been notified, and both Jane and Mrs. Gardiner were at Willow Hall.

She looked up from her paper. "I am writing to Mr. Darcy."

Mr. Abbot's smile was understanding. "Do not let us disturb you," was his only reply.

Aiden's response was not so accommodating. After trying to stand and take a step for what must have been the tenth time, he had dropped once again onto the floor. The situation did not please him, and he made his opinion about it known in a loud cry.

"We will go see if Cook has a biscuit, and then

it might be time for a visit to Mama." Mr. Abbot scooped up his son. The child's wails softened as he snuggled his head into his father's shoulder, his chubby arms clinging tightly to his papa.

Elizabeth turned back to her letter and began the task of telling Darcy about her sister's arrival with Wickham. She was just blowing her nose for the third time in only twice as many lines when her solitude was once again interrupted.

Mrs. Gardiner hurried into the room, stopped short, and looked very disconcerted to see Elizabeth.

"Is something the matter?" asked Elizabeth. Aunt Gardiner was typically unflappable. Even when Mama would take a spell of nerves, Aunt Gardiner could be counted on to tend to them with a smile and a soft voice. She was much like Jane in that way. But this morning, she looked very much like she could use a dose of Mama's salts.

Mrs. Gardiner sighed and dropped into a chair. "I had hoped when I heard someone in this room that it might be Lydia." She shook her head. "Unless she has taken herself out to the barn — which is an unlikely option — she is gone."

"Gone?" Elizabeth's heart leapt to her throat.

"Gone." Mrs. Gardiner's eyes filled with tears. "Her bed has not been slept in, and her travelling bag is missing with her."

Elizabeth rose and moved to look out the window and down the driveway to the lane beyond. "Where could she have gone? She knows no one, and her sense of direction is paltry at best." Her hand ran nervously from her elbow to her shoulder and back. There was one thing that would be worse than having Lydia married to Wickham, and that would be to have her lost forever.

Mrs. Gardiner shook her head in response. "I do not know."

"Mr. Wickham left with Mr. Williams, did he not?" Elizabeth asked, her letter forgotten.

"He did."

"And he would not return?"

"He holds no fondness for your sister," said her aunt.

"She is not in the barn or the stables," said Mr. Gardiner, coming into the room. "No horses have been taken, and there are no fresh marks on the driveway, nor has anyone heard anything unusual.

I have come to get a cup of tea, and then we will begin a search of the estate."

And so they did. After a cup of tea and a few fortifying bites of toast, as many of the party at Willow Hall as could be taken from their duties were gathered and a thorough search of the estate was conducted. No sign of Lydia, save a few footprints near the gate, could be found. And so, it was determined that Lydia had more than likely thought to follow the path of the road she had travelled to reach Willow Hall.

"I do not know what she is thinking," said Jane as she and Elizabeth travelled along the road toward Kympton.

"She was quite adamant that she not be forced to marry Mr. Wickham," said Aunt Gardiner. "My guess is that she is bound for Longbourn and her mother. We have only to check at Mr. Williams' to be certain that she has not gone there to beg Mr. Wickham to accompany her, and then we shall continue on to the coaching inn." She patted Jane's knee reassuringly. "The matter should be all settled before long."

Elizabeth did not miss the uncertainty in her aunt's countenance as Aunt Gardiner attempted to smile at her. With Lydia, nothing was ever settled easily. The logical path never seemed to be one that her sister ventured down. And then, if they were successful and found Lydia or discovered in which direction she had fled, there was still the issue of what to be done about her travelling with Wickham.

The gentlemen had taken horses so their travel to Mr. Williams' home was quicker than the carriage. So, before the ladies could reach where they would turn from the main road, Mr. Gardiner and Mr. Abbot had discovered what they needed to know and had turned back to find the carriage and direct it on to the coaching inn.

There, Mr. Abbot and Mr. Gardiner made inquiries, but to no avail. Lydia had not been seen by anyone, and with heavy hearts and at a slower pace than they had travelled previously, the party began their return to Willow Hall.

Chapter 13

Darcy paced the sitting room at Willow Hall while Mr. Bennet took a place at the window, watching for the return of his daughters. It had been Darcy's plan to stop only at Pemberley to refresh horses before continuing on to Scotland, but when Mr. Bennet had suggested stopping at Willow Hall to speak to Gardiner, Darcy had been happy to oblige as it meant he would have an opportunity to see Elizabeth. Upon arrival at Willow Hall, however, their plans had changed.

"Not gone to Scotland?" Mr. Bennet muttered for the third time since they had been told what news Mrs. Smith had regarding Lydia.

"So it appears," said Darcy.

Mr. Bennet shifted so that he could see Darcy. "Is there a way to inform the colonel of our change in plans?"

Darcy stopped mid-stride and turned to face Mr. Bennet. "Richard said he would stop at Pemberley." He furrowed his brow. "He may still be there."

His gaze fell on the writing-table. He might be able to send a message and keep Richard and Bingley from riding to Scotland unnecessarily. If he did not stop them at Pemberley, he would have to go after them, and that would take him away from Elizabeth yet again.

He sat down at the desk and lifted the letter which was only partially written to put it to the side. However, his eyes caught the name at the top of the page, and before he could pull them away, he had read the first few lines.

Mr. Darcy,

Forgive my impropriety in writing to you, but there is a disturbing matter which must be brought to your attention. I shall not dither about but shall come directly to the point. My sister, Lydia, has done something quite foolish and has travelled to Derbyshire in the company of Mr. Wickham.

Darcy pulled his eyes from the letter and lay it to the side as intended. Though he desired to read the remainder, he needed to send his message to Richard as quickly as possible. However, he promised himself, as soon as his task was done, he would return to the letter Elizabeth had been writing him.

"A messenger will be needed to carry this." Darcy placed a clean paper on the desk, giving Mr. Bennet the briefest of glances before setting about the business of writing to his cousin.

Before the ink was dry enough for the message to be folded, a lad from the stables had appeared. So, as he folded the message, Darcy gave instruction to the boy about its delivery.

Then, as Mr. Bennet returned to his position of watching at the window, Darcy picked up the letter he had placed to the side and continued reading.

Although her maid travelled with her, they spent more than one night on the road. It is my understanding that they were never parted while they travelled — not even to sleep. I am certain that you can see the gravity of this situation and that the solution for salvaging her reputation is for her to marry Mr. Wickham. However, she has not yet agreed to the arrangement. Indeed, both she and Mr. Wickham seem to be most vehemently opposed to such a suggestion. My uncle has written to my father, and we await his decision.

My heart is grieved not only at the foolishness of my sister and the life to which she is consigning herself but also for you and your sister. The thought of bringing such a man as Mr. Wickham into your family as a relation is nearly too awful to contemplate. To think that I should be the cause of such grief! It is overwhelming. And so, I release you from your promise. I cannot —

There was no more. The letter had been left incomplete, but the portion that was there struck panic in Darcy's heart. She was turning him away? He read it again and then a third time.

"No." He shook his head and stood. "She will not release me." He took up his hat. "I must find her."

Darcy was nearly at the stables before Mr. Bennet caught up to him.

"Elizabeth has broken the engagement?" he asked between laboured breaths.

Darcy handed Mr. Bennet the letter as he ordered a horse readied.

"It is incomplete," said Mr. Bennet to the back of the man in front of him.

"It is complete enough."

Mr. Bennet placed a hand on Darcy's shoulder. "It is never complete enough until the full matter has been told." He smiled gently when Darcy looked over his shoulder. "Allow her to finish her thoughts. They may not be as you assume." He handed the letter back to Darcy. "I will wait here, and I would suggest you do the same, but I am certain such a suggestion would not be heeded."

He chuckled at Darcy's expression. "No, a man violently in love is not one to sit idly by and wait." He removed his hand from Darcy's shoulder. "Be patient with her. Her tongue may be sharp, but her heart is tender." Then, he turned and ambled back toward the house.

Darcy tucked the letter into his pocket and mounted the horse that had been brought to him. With a cluck and a nudge, he urged the horse toward the road. Several minutes later, he drew to a stop before the parsonage.

"Philip," he called in greeting to the man, who was making his way towards him.

"Darcy, we had not expected to see you so soon." Philip looked nervously toward the house.

"Is she here?" Darcy asked. "Is Elizabeth here?"

He repeated when Philip did not respond immediately.

"She is." Philip stepped in front of his friend. "Some things have happened –."

"I know," Darcy pushed his way past Philip. "Which is why I must see her without delay."

Darcy hurried into the house. She would not release him from his promise. She would not refuse him again. He would make certain of it, and she could explain the rest of her letter after he had.

There were others in the room, but aside from Lucy, to whom he nodded a greeting, he was unsure of who they were, for he was looking for one person and one person only, and he had found her the instant he had entered.

"Mr. Darcy," Elizabeth said in surprise as he approached her.

He pulled the letter from his pocket. "You will not release me from my promise," he said. "I will not allow it, for I love you, Elizabeth Bennet. I would endure a connection to a thousand men such as Wickham for you."

"You would?" A smile spread across her face and relief washing through her spirit.

"I would if you will but say you will have me."

She nodded as tears formed in her eyes. "I will."

He turned toward Philip. "Call the banns," he said with a smile. Then, he turned his attention back to Elizabeth. "It seems I shall be marrying." And with that, he gathered Elizabeth into his arms and kissed her soundly.

~*~*~

"It is rarely who you expect," said Philip to Darcy later after all of the party from Willow Hall had left except Elizabeth, who had stayed behind at Lucy's request. Philip knew that it was an effort to give Darcy a few moments of calm before having to face the mix of delight and concern that would hang over Willow Hall. Large groups and high emotions had never been something with which Darcy had been comfortable.

Darcy shook his head. "She is not what I expected. She is far better."

"That is just how I feel about Lucy," agreed Philip. "God works in mysterious ways."

"That he does," agreed Mr. Harker from his chair. "I would not be surprised if the Good Lord provided a ram in the thicket for Miss Lydia."

Darcy shot him an inquisitive look.

"Faith, my lad. That is what trials test and

strengthen. Abraham was put to the test and just when the dire deed was to be completed, a ram was provided. And if the Lord could save Isaac from death, I believe He can save Miss Lydia from Wickham. Did He not save Lucy and Georgiana?"

"He did," Darcy acknowledged.

"Well, then," the elderly man pushed himself from his chair, "I shall go home and entreat the Lord for such a miracle."

He stopped in front of Darcy. "Miss Elizabeth seems a fine choice. Your mother and father would be pleased." He held out a hand which, though wrinkled, was steady and strong. "My joy to you both."

He clucked his tongue at Philip as the younger man stood to give his mentor assistance in exiting the house. "Mrs. Barnes will see me home, young man. You have guests."

Philip thought to protest, but from the set of Mr. Harker's jaw, he knew it would be to no avail. The gentleman's eyes might be growing dim, but his spirit of independence was not. So, he merely thanked him for his visit.

"You know, Darcy is a much better choice for her than your brother," Mr. Harker whispered as he waited for Lucy's aunt to say her farewells and join him. "And don't let your sister attempt to match Miss Bennet with Marcus either. She's a lovely girl, but far too tame. Marcus needs a wife with a bit of spirit." He chuckled. "Perhaps he can be the ram in the thicket," he said as he held out an arm to Mrs. Barnes.

Philip shook his head and sighed as he took his seat again.

"Mary Ellen truly was attempting to match Elizabeth with Marcus?" Darcy asked.

"Until you arrived," admitted Philip, "but Lucy set her straight after seeing how you greeted Miss Elizabeth."

"Has she attempted to match him with Miss Bennet?"

Philip shook his head. "He has shown no interest, so she has focused her work on our cousin — although I am not certain much encouragement is needed on either side."

Darcy's heart sank at the news. "Miss Bennet has shown interest in Harris?"

"Some." Philip studied his friend's expression. "Is there a reason Mary Ellen should not meddle?"

Darcy nodded slowly. "Bingley."

Philip scrubbed his hands down his face. "Maybe if Mary Ellen would marry, she would stop her interference with all her single relations."

"Should I speak to Richard then?" Darcy laughed at the surprise on Philip's face.

"You know?"

Darcy shrugged. "I do. It seems the only one who does not is my cousin."

Philip chuckled. "I suppose that is because she is not what he expects."

"She never is, is she?" Darcy asked, smiling at Elizabeth. He heard the crunch of gravel under horses' hooves and carriage wheels approach the house. "My carriage has arrived. I should see Elizabeth back to Willow Hall."

~*~*~

Elizabeth sat on the bench next to Darcy. He watched her nervously smooth her skirts. Her cheeks were flushed a lovely rose colour.

"I know it is not entirely proper," he began, trying to help her feel at ease.

She shook her head. "No, it is not." She smiled at him impertinently. "But neither is kissing a gentleman in public, and I have already done that today."

"And I hope you might kiss him again in private."

Her cheeks grew even rosier. "I would like that," her admission was barely above a whisper.

He slid closer to her and bent his mouth to hers, kissing her softly at first and then more firmly as he wrapped her in his embrace. Breaking their kiss, he held her close and enjoyed her presence in his arms before he spoke of the letter.

"You thought I was sending you away?"

He nodded. "But your father told me that my assumption might not be true."

"Yet, you accused me of that very thing at the parsonage." She peeked up at him. "Explain yourself, sir."

He kissed her upturned forehead. "I decided it did not matter how you were to conclude that letter. I was going to make certain you could not refuse me."

"So you professed your love for me in the sitting room at a parsonage."

He chuckled. "Yes. Not that it was the first time I have done so."

She squeezed him tight. "I can never apologize enough for how I refused you. It is why I was not going to refuse you in that letter. I lost you once through my foolishness. I would not be the one to send you away again. I released you from our agreement so that you might choose without fear of breaking your promise to me." She looked up at him again. "I hoped you would choose me, but . . ."

"Knowing what you know of my relationship with Wickham, you would not force me to be tied to him."

She nodded. "I could not bear the thought of your growing to despise me for the connection."

He tipped her chin up so that he could kiss her once again. "I will see him well-situated and your sister as safe as can be, and I will do so gladly as long as you are mine."

"You are too good," she said. "You are not what I expected."

"Nor are you what I expected." He smiled down at her. "But Philip assures me that that is how it is with love. And I do love you, Elizabeth Bennet."

"And I love you, Fitzwilliam Darcy," she said stretching up to kiss him.

And so the unlikely pair — he, the nephew of an earl and master of a grand estate, and she, the daughter of a country gentleman and his tenant's guest — passed the last few miles to Willow Hall wrapped in each other's arms, speaking in word and deed of their love for each other, and knowing that, come what may, they had found their happiness both now and forever.

Before You Go

If you enjoyed this book, be sure to let others
know by leaving a review.

~*~*~

Want to know when other books in this series
will be available?
You can always know what's new with my
books by subscribing to my mailing list.
(There will, of course, be a thank you gift for
joining because I think my readers are awesome!)
Book News from Leenie Brown
(bit.ly/LeenieBBookNews)

~*~*~

Turn the page to read an excerpt from *So Very
Unexpected*, Book Three in the Willow Hall series.

So Very Unexpected Excerpt

The next book in the Willow Hall series is So Very Unexpected. This book begins at Lydia's unexpected arrival at Willow Hall. She's not marrying Wickham. She absolutely isn't — and she'll do whatever she needs to do to avoid it.

CHAPTER 1

Lydia Bennet pulled the door to Willow Hall closed as quietly as she could. She did not want to wake a single person, especially her uncle. Marry Wickham? A lieutenant? A man who cheated and played cards far too often? Did her uncle wish for her to be a pauper? She knew she was not made for such lowly circumstances. Did Uncle Gardiner not also know? If she married Wickham, she might be limited to just one maid of all work! Lydia shuddered at the thought.

Reaching the gate, she turned to take one last look at Willow Hall and then, biting her lip, continued on to the road. Her heart beat loudly in her chest. She had done some things before which required a good dose of fortitude, but none as daring as this. Above her, the moon was only a sliver and clouds blocked many of the stars. Lydia stood looking down the road one way and then the other for a few minutes. Surely, the carriage that brought her to Willow Hall had turned left into the driveway, or was it right? She sighed and crouched down to look more closely at the ground. It was no use; there were groves from carriages both to her right and to her left. With a shrug, she swallowed her fear and turned in the direction her mind had first told her must be the way to Kympton.

She felt a need to whistle to fill the silence of the night, but she dared not. She would do nothing to draw attention to herself from anyone or anything. The thought sent a shiver down her spine. This was foolish and far too dangerous. She paused, turned back, and then remembering her uncle's words, "It must be done. You must marry him to

save both your reputation and that of your family."
She turned away from Willow Hall once again and
continued on her way.

For the next twenty minutes, she entertained
herself with thoughts of ribbons, lace, and
bonnets, describing to herself the perfect hat to
accompany the new yellow dress she would have
when she reached home. Mama would see to it.
Lydia smiled to herself. Mama always saw to what
Lydia wanted even when Papa was reticent. Mama
would not see her married to a lieutenant. A
captain was the lowest rank of which Mama, and
truly anyone of sense, would find acceptable. A
lieutenant's wife! Indeed! Lydia nearly laughed at
the thought until she heard something — a
scurrying beside the road to her right. Something
very like a fit of nerves gripped her heart. Not
wishing to be preyed on by either man or beast,
Lydia scooted off the road and into the stand of
trees on the left. The woods indeed felt safer. She
picked her way between the trees not entirely sure
if she was still travelling in the same direction as
she had intended, but going back toward that
scurrying sound was not an option.

After another twenty minutes of walking and

feeling quite turned about and tired, Lydia spotted a cottage. It was a tiny stone cottage with a small structure for storage next to it. Perhaps she could rest there and be tucked away from the notice of any night creatures. She just wished a moment to rest so that this feeling of being utterly lost would vanish.

She rapped lightly on the door to the storage building. She lay her ear against the wood, and after a few minutes of listening intently and hearing no sounds, she opened the door. The structure housed nothing — not a scythe, not a rake, not a bucket. There were no flowers or herbs hanging from the rafters to dry. It was empty. Completely and entirely empty. Lydia studied the perplexing emptiness for a moment before finding a corner and sitting down with her feet tucked beneath her and her head resting, at first, tentatively and then more fully leaning into the wall as she relaxed.

The first rays of sun poked their fingers through a small gap between two boards on the wall opposite Lydia. The light played with her hair and then crept across her face, tickling first her nose and then her eyelashes. Lydia swatted at the offending light and turned her head to avoid it. Her hair caught on a nail that had not been hammered in completely, and the sharp pain of the tugging woke her. She rubbed her eyes and looked around the shed. In the light of the morning, it was not quite as empty as it had been in the lantern light. In one corner, there were five pieces of wood neatly stacked, but that was all — five pieces of wood and a lot of nothing else.

She peeked out the door. There was neither the smell of a fire nor a wisp of smoke rising from the chimney of the cottage. Confident she was alone, she stepped out of her sleeping spot and surveyed her surroundings. Nothing looked familiar. There were fields of grass and flowers beyond the cottage and trees behind her. To her left was a slope that descended for some distance. She had not seen any of this when they had travelled from Kympton to Willow Hall. She would have remembered it, for it was beautiful — the kind of beautiful that caused one to stop and admire it for hours, the kind of beautiful that inspired paintings and poems, the kind of beautiful that brought a smile to her face and peace to her heart.

After several minutes of admiring her

surroundings, Lydia decided it was time to explore the cottage. Carefully, she opened the door, calling out a greeting as she did, just in case someone might be within. She waited for a reply, and when none came, she entered. Dust covered the table and the three glasses that sat turned upside down on the small cabinet next to a larger cupboard with doors. In the small sitting room, Lydia took a seat on a large chair in front of the fireplace. The back of the chair wrapped up and around her. She leaned her head against its back. Ah, she sighed with pleasure. Even though the fabric of the chair was worn so thin that the pattern was little more than a shadow, this would have been much more comfortable than that shed.

She allowed herself to close her eyes and enjoy the comfort for what she thought was a moment. However, when one is as tired from travelling in crowded coaches, debating with one's relative to avoid an untenable marriage, and then walking for nearly an hour in a circular path along a road and amongst trees while fearing that some creature was going to attack you, even a moment of rest can stretch into hours.

Lydia's weary body welcomed sleep, and just as it

had in the shed, it did not wake of its own accord. However, this time it was not the gentle and playful fingers of the sun which woke Lydia but the banging of a door and a masculine voice.

Lydia tucked herself into the chair as best she could. The back of the chair was nearly turned completely toward the door, so perhaps if she were very still, she would not be noticed. She sucked in her breath and closed her eyes as she listened to the sound of boots thumping through the cottage.

Marcus Dobney peered into all the rooms in the cottage and was about to lock the door and leave when he heard a small, muffled sneeze from the sitting room. He shook his head. He had looked in that room and seen no one. Another sneeze. Ah, the chair by the fireplace! How had he neglected to check there?

He crept into the room, coming up behind the chair. "I heard you sneeze," he said as he stood behind the chair and looked down at the occupant. "Miss Lydia?" he asked in surprise as she squealed and shot to her feet.

She whirled on him. "That was not nice. You frightened me half to death." She placed her hands on her hips and glared at the intruder, who looked oddly familiar. "How do you know my name?"

He chuckled and leaned on the back of the chair. "It is also not nice to be stealing into cottages that do not belong to you." He tipped his head and smirked as her eyes narrowed. She looked as defiant now as she had last evening when they had been introduced. "You do not remember me?"

Lydia shook her head, but then her brows furrowed, and her mouth formed a perfect oh as her eyes grew wide as she began to recall why the fine looking gentleman leaning on the back of the tired old chair looked so familiar. "You were with Captain Harris." She bit her lip as she strained to remember his name. To be honest, she had not been focused on much yesterday except convincing her uncle that she did not need to marry Wickham. There had been two gentlemen who had come to call, and then Jane escorted them to the garden to find Miss Dobney. That was it! "Mr. Dobney, is it?" Lydia fluttered her lashes just a bit and smiled sweetly. Most of the men she had met responded well to such an expression.

Marcus nodded and motioned for Lydia to be seated on the settee near the window as he pulled the chair to face it. "Why are you here in my cottage when you should be at Willow Hall?"

Lydia watched his fingers unbutton his jacket as he sunk into the chair and swung one leg over the other. This was his cottage? Her brow furrowed once again. Surely, a man, who wore such beautiful clothes, did not live in this tiny dust-covered cottage. "You live here?"

He chuckled again. It was a sound that Lydia found dreadfully infuriating. There was no need to laugh at her for asking a simple question.

"No, I do not live here, but just the same, the cottage is mine — or will be when I come into my inheritance." He leaned forward. "Now, tell me why I should not call the constable to report a vagrant?"

Lydia pulled herself up and looked down her nose at the man across from her. "I am not a vagrant. I merely needed a place to rest, and the door was unlocked." She folded her arms. "It seems very careless of you to leave your inheritance unlocked."

He chuckled again, and she huffed. "My steward forgot to lock it yesterday when he was checking on the fields. That is why I am here. I told him I would see to it."

"It is not well-tended," she muttered.

He raised a brow at the comment but let it pass. "You are avoiding my question."

She smiled at him again and rose from her seat. "I am sorry, but I must be on my way. If you could just point me in the direction of Kympton."

This time he laughed out loud. "Sit down."

If she were not so irritated with him, she might have taken a moment to admire his smile. It was very nice. Very nice, indeed. But she was not in a mood to admire his pleasant mouth or his lovely brown eyes that were currently sparkling with amusement.

He pointed to the settee, and she sat. "You were going to Kympton?"

"I may have gotten turned about in the woods," she admitted.

"You most certainly did," he replied.

"It was dark," she mumbled.

His eyes grew wide. "You were travelling at night?"

"Of course," she smoothed her skirts so she would not have to look at his face. It was a handsome face and wearing an expression she particularly did not like — especially on a handsome face. Handsome men were to look at her with interest, of course, but not as he was. His expression was one that spoke of him wondering quite loudly about her mental abilities. "It is far easier to make an unnoticed exit when it is dark and everyone is asleep." She skewered him with a challenging look. "I do not suppose you remember doing anything so exciting in your youth?" There, that ought to grate, but just to make certain it did –"Not that I am calling you old, per se." She smiled and fluttered her lashes. "I am just saying you are not young." The effect was as she had hoped. His smile faded, and his eyes narrowed. Displeasure she could allow on a handsome face.

"I was never so foolish in my youth."

She shrugged.

He could see the anger at his comment by the set of her mouth and the narrowing of her eyes. Mary Ellen would often respond in such a fashion when she did not wish to continue a particular discussion.

"Now, tell me why a girl," he emphasized the word, enjoying the darkening in her eyes, "like you is sneaking off in the night? A secret rendezvous? Perhaps with Wickham?" He attempted to keep his tone from growling the name, but his success was only limited.

She shot to her feet, grabbed her bag, and would have left if Marcus had not blocked her path.

She stepped close to him, so close that she had to tip her head up to glare at him. "I am not a girl!"

He swallowed as he looked down at her. Her figure was definitely not girlish. However, the stamp of her foot was.

"And I do not know why everyone insists that I would even consider a man like Mr. Wickham." She visibly shuddered as she said his name.

"Perhaps it is because, as I have heard tell, you flirted with him in Brighton and then travelled with him for several days." He folded his arms across his chest in an attempt to avoid seeing any more of her than her face when he looked down. She rolled her large hazel eyes at him and pursed her lovely lips causing him to swallow once again.

"As I explained to my uncle, a man such as Mr. Wickham is easily led. A mention of exposing his swindling to the ones he has played for fools and a hint that a rumour of doing harm to me might reach Mr. Darcy ensured me safe passage."

"A lady is never safe with a man like Wickham," growled Marcus.

Her eyes sparkled at the comment — most fetchingly he thought.

"So, I am now a lady?" She smiled at him and raised an eyebrow. Then, swiftly, she took a step to her right and scooted past him. "I really must be on my way, for as you say, no lady is safe with a man such as Wickham, so it is best that I do not remain where I might be forced to be tied to him in marriage." She threw the words over her shoulder as she hurried to the door of the cottage.

Marcus chased after her and grabbed her by an elbow. "You are not leaving. You are returning to Willow Hall. Your family must be worried."

She wrenched her arm free. "I am not returning to Willow Hall!"

He reached for her arm once again, but she pulled it away. "You are," he said as he took two long strides to catch up to her again.

"No. I am not." She began to run.

"You are being a fool."

"I will not marry him, Mr. Dobney. I will not!"

He sighed and ran after her. "Perhaps, but you must return to your family." He pulled her bag from her hand and sat it on the ground behind him.

"Give me my bag!"

"No, not until you are at Willow Hall."

"Oh, you are infuriating."

He smiled as she stamped her foot.

"Very well, I shall go to Willow Hall with you, but I am not staying."

"Yes, you are." He chuckled at her scowl. "You are a rather adorable girl even when you are put out." He called to his horse. "I will need a way to get home," he explained.

"I am not a girl," she muttered as she stood there waiting for him to tie her bag onto his horse.

"And I am not old," he retorted and began walking with Lydia scampering behind trying to keep pace with his long strides.

Acknowledgements

There are many who have had a part in the creation of this story. Some have read and commented on it. Some have proofread for grammatical errors and plot holes. Others have not even read the story (and a few, I know, will never read it), but their encouragement and belief in my ability, as well as their patience when I became cranky or when supper was late or the groceries ran low, was invaluable.

And so, I would like to say *thank you* to Zoe, Rose, Betty, Regina, Kristine, Ben, and Kyle, as well as the lovely readers at darcyandlizzy.com. I feel blessed through your help, support, and understanding.

I have not listed my dear husband in the above group because, to me, he deserves his own special thank you, for without his somewhat pushy insistence that I start sharing my writing, none of my writing goals and dreams would have been met.

Other Leenie B Books

You can find all of Leenie's books at this link
bit.ly/LeenieBBooks
where you can explore the collections below

~*~

Other Pens, Mansfield Park

~*~

Touches of Austen Collection

~*~

Other Pens, Pride and Prejudice

~*~

Dash of Darcy and Companions Collection

~*~

Marrying Elizabeth Series

~*~

Willow Hall Romances

~*~

The Choices Series

~*~

Darcy Family Holidays

~*~

Darcy and... An Austen-Inspired Collection

About the Author

Leenie Brown has always been a girl with an active imagination, which, while growing up, was both an asset, providing many hours of fun as she played out stories, and a liability, when her older sister and aunt would tell her frightening tales. At one time, they had her convinced Dracula lived in the trunk at the end of the bed she slept in when visiting her grandparents!

Although it has been years since she cowered in her bed in her grandparents' basement, she still has an imagination which occasionally runs away with her, and she feeds it now as she did then — by reading!

Her heroes, when growing up, were authors, and the worlds they painted with words were (and still are) her favourite playgrounds! Now, as an adult, she spends much of her time in the Regency world, playing with the characters from her favourite Jane Austen novels and those of her own creation.

When she is not traipsing down a trail in an attempt to keep up with her imagination, Leenie resides in the beautiful province of Nova Scotia with her two sons and her very own Mr. Brown (a wonderful mix of all the best of Darcy, Bingley, and Edmund with a healthy dose of the teasing Mr. Tilney and just a dash of the scolding Mr. Knightley).

Connect with Leenie Brown

E-mail:
LeenieBrownAuthor@gmail.com
Facebook:
www.facebook.com/LeenieBrownAuthor
Blog:
leeniebrown.com
Patreon:
https://www.patreon.com/LeenieBrown
Subscribe to Leenie's Mailing List:
Book News from Leenie Brown
(bit.ly/LeenieBBookNews)

Manufactured by Amazon.ca
Bolton, ON